Adrianna Swift Series

SWIFT

SNAKE

N. L.

Book 2
Written by N L Hiser

The Adrianna Swift Series

Swift Snake

N.L. Hiser

Copyright 2021

ISBN

All rights reserved. For information go to https://www.nlhiserwrites.com.

Cover created by N L Hiser Writes

Indie published by N L Hiser Writes

Adrianna Swift Series Book 2

Edition 1

Book 2
Written by N L Hiser

For anyone suffering from PTSD, trauma, depression, anxiety, panic attacks, suicidal thoughts, or abuse.

You are not alone. Find your reason to fight. We need you here.

This book is dedicated to you and your strength.

The Adrianna Swift Series
Swift Snake

Book 2
Written by N L Hiser

<u>One</u>

The stench of blood and embalming fluid filled Adrianna's nostrils. She scrunched up her nose, knowing it wasn't a smell she was likely to forget. She looked over her shoulder to the mortician as he talked to the cop by the doors. The doctor's age, while showing in his silver locks and small lines engraved in his face, moved with sureness and of a youthful grace. Though he spent long hours standing bent over corpses, he seemed in better shape than most. His height reined over the young cop, only making the man apologize faster. Apparently, he had messed up some paperwork.

He must be a rooky, Adrianna mused. She let her gaze go back to the body in front of her. She had refused to be out of view of the coroner's truck the entire ride back to Staten Island. Though dead, the Staten Island Stalker still seemed to wear his malicious sneer. It seemed, even in death, he received pleasure from being a fucking psychopath.

The doors behind her opened as Detective Jones and his wife walked into the morgue. "She shouldn't be in here, Jones." The doctor said as he walked over, nonchalantly dismissing the rooky.

"She refused to stay home." Jones muttered softly, as they walked over to the second metal table.

"Mrs. Jones, you really don't want to see him like this." He mentioned gently, as Adrianna stepped up to the table.

"We've known him for years. I couldn't let my husband come alone. Besides," the woman's voice dropped to nearly a whisper as a tear glided down her cheek. "He's family."

Adrianna saw tears well up in the Jones' eyes again. "Did you tell her?" She whispered lightly, knowing that the woman was sure to break down in a moment.

Jones shook his head as his tears fell freely. "I-I couldn't."

Adrianna exchanged a glance with the doctor before he bowed his head. "Ma'am, Detective Brenner was shot with a rifle at point blank range," Jones clasped his wife's hand consolingly. "I'm sorry, but he was shot in the back." The realization of how Alex may look hit the woman, freezing her to the core.

Adrianna could see the woman's resolve return to her, as she straightened and took hold of her husband. The men had been partners and best friends for years. Adrianna could tell by the determined look in the woman's eyes, that she would grieve alone later and had already decided to be there for her husband instead. "It's alright." She replied, iron in her voice. "We must say our goodbyes and give him our respects."

In that moment, Adrianna knew she liked and respected Jones' wife. She was a woman to be revered. Adrianna pushed back her shoulders and nodded to the doctor. His eyes are crestfallen, but he gently pulled back the white sheet, revealing Alex's body. He had a peaceful look on his face, on Adrianna was thankful for. Just below his neck, a gaping hole had formed from the bullet's exit. Suddenly, she realized she was lucky it hadn't hit her. Somehow, Alex had protected her with his life and his death. Her stomach twisted, and she suddenly had the urge to retch. She took a deep, steadying breath and forced the tears in her eyes to stop running and glanced over to Mrs. Jones.

Tears ran freely down her cheeks as her red, swollen eyes resorted to blinking them away. She wrapped her arm around her husband, pulled his gaze from his partner's body, and pulled his head onto her shoulder. He sobbed uncontrollably into her shirt as she consoled him, but her voice never wavered. The doctor replaced the sheet and silently walked away to his desk on the other end of the room.

Adrianna softly squeezed Alex's cold hand, and whispered, "Goodbye, Alex." A tear slid down her cheek and splashed onto the sheet. Unable to hold it back any longer, she turned to slip away quietly, to leave the Jones' alone and to be alone in her own thoughts.

"Wait." She turned to see Mrs. Jones looking at her. Her husband lifted his head and watched the women. "Thank you."

"I don't understand." Adrianna uttered quietly, confused.

The woman looked over at the Stalker's sheeted body on the next table. "I know you did it for your family, and for everything he put you through. But..." she paused and looked back to Alex. "Thank you. You avenged Alex, and everyone else that he hurt, too. You ended this nightmare."

"I thought I did." She replied soberly. "But it's not over yet." A corner of her mouth twisted up in a reassuring smile before she then turned to leave, glancing one last time at the Stalker's body. "But it will be soon." She whispered as she strode out of the double doors.

Book 2
Written by N L Hiser

<u>Two</u>

S
he made her way back upstairs to the main floor and headed towards the restrooms, passing officers and detectives at their desks, and going about their duties. A few glanced up at her when she walked past, but none spoke. They didn't have to.

Finally alone, she closed the bathroom door behind her. She bent over the sink and instantly broke into sobs as her emotions took hold of her. Her mind raced. Why him? Why not me? The bastard already took everything from me. Alex shouldn't have jumped in front of me. He should've let me die. They could've taken him after that. He didn't deserve to die! She cried. It should've been me. Not him. Not Alex! And now there's a partner out there somewhere? What am I supposed to do? What if I can't find him? What if we can't stop him before he kills someone else? Or before he disappears for good? What am I supposed to do?

She slid down to the floor and put her head on her knees and tried to stop thinking and stop crying. She tried to still herself and took a deep breath, but instead burst into a blubbering mess.

Her breath came faster, and her heartbeat quickened. Sweat beaded on her forehead. She could feel heat rise to her neck as if she were having a hot flash.

Suddenly, a tall dark-haired woman walked through the door into the bathroom. Seeing Adrianna on the floor crying, she immediately closed the door behind her and walked over. "Honey, are you alright?"

Adrianna looked up, surprised. "Oh, yes. Yes, I'm alright. I'm just having a panic attack. I'm sorry." She gasped.

"Oh honey, don't be sorry. I have them too." The woman offered in a husky voice. She glanced around the bathroom and self-consciously rubbed the knot on her throat. "Don't get embarrassed. Would you like me to sit and talk with you until it passes?"

"You don't have to. I know you have work to do." She whispered. "I don't want to be a bother."

"Oh, please. You're fine." She sat down next to Adrianna, smiling. "It depends on how bad of an anxiety attack I'm having, but most of the time it helps me to have someone to talk to. You know, something to distract the mind. But whatever works for you. We can talk, or I can just sit here and be with you. Sometimes that's all a girl needs, time."

Adrianna couldn't help but smile a little. "Thank you. Yeah, I'd like to talk. Just about anything else than what's going on downstairs."

"Alright. I'm Christy, by the way." Settling in beside her she continued. "So, have you watched any good movies lately?"

"No, I haven't." a small laugh rose in her throat. "Have you? I haven't been to the movies in a long time."

"My friends and I go to the movies almost every weekend. You should come. It's a lot of fun. We watched this one Saturday, about this girl that

The Adrianna Swift Series
Swift Snake

had one of those smart houses. The damn house turned against her! It locked her in and all kinds of shit. You won't find my ass in one of those smart houses. I didn't know they could do all that."

"That's crazy. Yeah, whoever came up with them went way too far. I know we needed technology to get better, but it's all went way too far. They should've stopped years ago. Even the damn cell phones. Why didn't they stop 'upgrading' everything about fifteen years ago, and instead, perfect what they had? Every one of them have glitches and problems in one way or another. They should've just stopped and found a way to fix the ones they already made, instead of inventing the next new thing for your phone." Breathing easier and feeling her strength come back, Adrianna took a deep, calming breathe.

"Very true. How are you feeling?"

"Better. Thanks. Please don't tell anyone about this. I don't want everyone out there to think I'm weak."

"Honey, having a panic attack does not make you weak. I've had them since I was a kid. If anything, they make you stronger. You understand,

and you find somehow to adapt and eventually, move on. There's a lot of strength in that. It took me a long time to see it too, but it's the truth. I know what all you've been through." She eyed Adrianna cautiously, unaware of how she'd react to being so forthcoming. "You've had to suffer through so much. And yet, you're not a victim, you never backed down, and you never gave up. Don't ever think you're weak. You're one of the strongest women I've ever met."

"Thanks. You are too. To have gone through what you have and be a cop, I know it wasn't easy. But there's a lot of people who would argue that you're wrong about me. Besides, I don't feel strong. Especially during a panic attack." She breathed.

"Well, there's always going to be someone fighting against you. Always someone trying to beat you down." Standing, she continued. "And you know what? Fuck them. Let their bullshit fuel you to get better and better at everything you do. Let them know who the fuck they're dealing with." She squeezed Adrianna's hands and pulled her to her feet. "Now, clean yourself up and stand tall. Then, you go handle your business."

The Adrianna Swift Series
Swift Snake

With that, she smiled, checked herself in the mirror smiling at herself, and walked out of the bathroom before Adrianna could say another word. Smiling, she silently thanked the woman. She turned back to the mirror in front of her and leaned over to splash her face. After drying off, she straightened herself up and walked outside.

She walked back to all the desks and found Jones sitting at his, staring into space. Forcing herself to push her shoulders back and stand tall, she walked over. "Jones?"

"Hmm?"

"Jones."

He finally looked up at her, somewhat surprised. "Oh, I'm sorry."

"Don't be. Where's your wife?"

"She went home."

"Oh, alright then. Did the blood test come back?"

"They won't be done for two weeks."

"What? Can't they rush them or something? I mean, he is a serial killer!"

"I know. I already sent the request up, but that's ultimately up to the chief. And even with the rush, his prints don't match anyone in the system, just his past victims. What makes you think his blood will?"

"Maybe he's managed to keep from being fingerprinted. But I doubt that he's never been to the hospital. Even when you're born, they run your blood and everything." Jones shrugged; his hands tied. "Where's the chief?"

"No. We don't do things like that." He said sternly. "I sent the request up the chain to the chief. We have to wait."

"I don't have time to wait." Adrianna spun around and headed to the only enclosed office she could see, reckoning it'd be the Chief's. She could hear Jones jump up and run after her, but she didn't care. There wasn't any time to waste.

Coming up to the door to his office, and seeing the Chief inside doing paperwork, she turned the knob and let herself in. "Chief?"

The Adrianna Swift Series
Swift Snake

"Yes…?" he asked as he raised his eyes from the paper he was reading.

"We need a rush on those blood tests on the Stalker." Jones walked into the room behind her, just as the last word slid from her mouth.

"Well this is very unorthodox. Ms. Davidson-."

"It's Swift now. I changed my name back to Adrianna Swift when I left town."

"Oh, yes. Brenner told me. Ms. Swift, you can't just come in here and tell me you need a rush on the lab results. You're not even supposed to be here."

"Chief, I'm not leaving until I know who the partner is. I'm in danger as long as he's out there, and so is everyone else."

Pausing for a moment, deciding what to say, he replied. "Detective Jones' request is right here. I was already going to approve it, Ms. Swift. We will let you know when we get the results in and as soon as we get a name on the partner. You must let us do our jobs. Jones go home. Take a few days off. You shouldn't be here either."

"But Chief, I want to stay and-."

"No. Jones, that wasn't a request." The Chief's eyes softened a bit looking at Jones. "We can't do anything else for him right now. Go home."

With that, he signed the request and continued to the next stack of papers to go through, silently dismissing them. Disgruntled, Adrianna turned and left the office. Knowing full well she wasn't leaving, she resigned to find another way.

"Adrianna, wait." Jones hurried up beside her. "What were you thinking? You know you could've gotten me in trouble with the Chief! What are you doing?"

"Are you going to help me or not?" she looked at him quizzically.

He stared at her, unsure what to do. "Fine. You know I want this guy too. But we got to do it the right way." Thinking, he said "Meet me by the car in five minutes. We have to leave anyways, might as well take our work with us."

Adrianna nodded and gathered her things as Jones disappeared down the hall. Five minutes later, he sidled out the front doors toward the car with two brown boxes.

"Get in. I got all the files for the Stalker case, so we can go through them."

Adrianna slid into the passenger seat. "Where are we going?"

<u>Three</u>

They were quiet during the ride. Adrianna found herself watching the houses pass and the leaves dance along the streets as the wind blew through them. Christmas lights were already being put up on the street posts through town, and wreaths adorned most of the houses from doors. Thanksgiving was only a few weeks away, and it seemed everyone was skipping it as usual.

She placed her hand on the door to roll down the window a little bit and let the autumn breeze hit her face. But, when she did, her fingers touched something in the door handle. Curious, she looked down and raised it closer to her face to see. Inside a tiny white envelope was a small key and a sliver of paper that read, *Brenner.*

"What's this?" she asked Jones.

He glanced over to her, and realization dawned on him. Quietly, he replied. "That's Alex's spare house key. He kept it there in case he needed it." Smiling a little, he continued. "He always said it was there for me, too. If I ever needed a place to stay."

Adrianna looked at the key, with the little sliver of paper, and wished Alex were with them. Silently, she put the key back in the envelope and placed it back in the door handle. She held the piece of paper in her palm and closed her fingers around it. I miss you Alex, she thought. You'd know what to do next.

"I have to go to his house in the morning, to get his outfit and try to find his documents for the lawyers. I...don't really want to go over there by myself. I know it'll be hard on you too, but I would really appreciate the company." His voice shook. His brown eyes looked tired and stressed. She knew it was hard on him asking for help and couldn't find it in her to let him down.

"Okay." A tear pooled in her eye, threatening to slide out. "I'd like to go."

Silence once again invaded the car, both afraid to talk for crying. Adrianna glanced around the inside of the cruiser. Of course, Alex would still have some of his things in the car, she hadn't thought of it until then. Without wanting to seem nosey though, she continued gazing out the window.

A moment later, they pulled into a small driveway. The house was quaint with large picture windows. The white paint was peeling in areas, no doubt from lack of time for maintenance. The chimney billowed grey white smoke, hinting at a warm and cozy atmosphere. The lights glowed through the windows, beckoning them inside to warm up.

"Whose house is this?" she asked.

He chuckled as he lifted the boxes into his arms. "Mine of course. Now come on in. Dinner's almost ready. Oh, and don't mind the wife. She's a little pushy when it comes to guests. She just tries a little too much to make everyone comfortable. Come on!" He led the way to the front door and gestured her inside.

"Oh, um, thank you." She smiled.

The Adrianna Swift Series
Swift Snake

Jones walked in behind her and closed the door. After putting the boxes down, he took their coats and hung them in the closet. "Sam? Is that you?" Mrs. Jones rang through the house.

"Yeah, it's me." He smiled at Adrianna and whispered, "She should be glad it's me. The woman always forgets to lock the door." He giggled, shaking his head.

"I heard that." Mrs. Jones said, as she walked in from the kitchen. Sam's eyes shot over to her, wide like a schoolboy caught with his finger in the cake. Noticing Adrianna, her expression changed to worry. "Is everything alright?"

"Oh, yeah. Detective Jones-."

"Call me Sam." He interjected.

"Sam invited me for dinner. I hope that's alright."

"Oh, of course dear. Come on in and make yourself comfortable. Dinner will be done in just a minute." She smiled. Turning to return to the kitchen she hurriedly added, "And you can call me Iris."

"Thank you."

"Now," said Sam, turning to Adrianna. "Your bags are still in the car. You will stay here tonight and for however long you stay in town. I don't know if you plan on moving back here after everything is over, or if you will go back to Luray, but you will be safe here. Plus, we can work on the case. Since I'm off for a few days, I'll be here most of the time too."

"I can't stay here. That's putting your wife in danger, Sam. It's better if I just go to a hotel."

"And worry about being alone when that bastard shows? No. You'll stay here. Besides my wife can hold her own. We've been through situations like this. Not as extreme, but you can count on her."

"Yes, you can. Besides, we're stronger together. And Alex loved you. That makes you family. No matter what." The woman added as she strolled back into the room.

"Does that mean you know about the case?"

"Oh yeah." Sam answered for his wife. "We found out years ago, it was better, and safer for the kids and Iris, if she knew the details. If some stuff's going down, I tell her."

"Plus, he's not very good at lying to me." She winked.

"Only because I never *want* to lie to you, baby." Sam kissed her on the cheek, smiling.

"I know." Iris grinned. "Now come on in for some dinner. I hope you like meatloaf." She looped her arm through Adrianna's and lead her to the dining room.

"I love meatloaf." She smiled. Sam brought Adrianna's bags in from the car and joined them in the dining room.

<u>Four</u>

After dinner, Adrianna and Sam **sat** at the table perusing the case files. She could hear Iris washing dishes in the kitchen, humming to herself. She smiled slightly and picked up the next folder.

"Wait." Sam put his hand on the folder to stop her from opening it.

"What is it?" Her head slightly tilted in curiosity.

"It's your file. I don't know if you really want to see that."

"Oh." She thought about it for a moment and then asked, "What's all inside it?"

"Paperwork and files mostly. But your hospital and crime scene photos are in there, too."

Iris appeared in the doorway of the kitchen, watching to see what she'd do. Taking a deep breathe, she opened the folder. Inside was her summary file, detailing her height, weight, age, et cetera.

Next was the crime scene photos of her home, the blood, her husband, and daughter. She took another deep breath, willing herself not to cry as she looked at the picture of her daughter. She forced herself to move on and saw photos of herself when the police had found her in the warehouse, and then more from the hospital when she was taken in.

"I've never seen these pictures. I can't believe I looked-."

"I know. When we first found you in the warehouse, you were unconscious. I don't know if the doctors ever told you, but you died twice on the way to the hospital. None of us thought you'd live. When we got word at the station from the hospital, that you pulled out of surgery and was stable, everyone was shocked and incredibly happy."

"It was all over the news. Some dumbass even snuck a photo of you from your hospital room and the press got a hold of it. It was awful. Nobody could believe you had survived such torture. It was a miracle." Iris paused as Adrianna continued to look at the photos. "Now, you're sitting here in our dining room, and you look healthier than you did in the before picture here." She smiled, pointing at the small photo attached to her file.

"When I decided to leave Staten Island, I was running. But after I met a friend, I realized I had to become stronger and be able to defend myself. I didn't even know I had this big cut here." She pointed to her cheek in the hospital photo. "I can't even see it now." Her fingertips grazed her cheek, feeling to see if she could find the scar.

"You had an excellent doctor." Iris said. She turned and went back to finish the dishes.

Once her humming resumed, Sam asked, "So, how are you?" Adrianna looked up from the photos, raising a brow at him. "You know what I mean. You've left Staten Island and went states away, building a wall against anyone that comes knocking. Then he breaks out of prison and comes after you. And if that isn't enough, he killed Alex and you killed him. I know you're going through some craziness in your head right now. So, come out with it. How are you?"

The Adrianna Swift Series
Swift Snake

"I'm not here for therapy." She closed her folder and slid it a pile.

"No. You're here because this horrible crap happened to you. And you're here because you're trying to find out whoever's doing this and kill them too. Now, I'm with you. Otherwise, I wouldn't have brought you here and I wouldn't be letting you go through these files with me. I know you want to catch him. And we will. One way or another, dead or alive. I don't care. He killed my partner and best friend. But if we're going to work on this together, I need to know you're okay and that you can handle whatever happens. I need to know I can count on you not to go rogue." His brown eyes bored into hers as his brows furrowed.

She sighed. "Look, I can't promise that I won't freak out. I have been freaking out. Ever since he…ever since that night, I've had nightmares and anxiety attacks. I've been paranoid. They're getting better, and I am learning how to cope with them, but I can't promise I won't freak out and have another one. I can promise though, I won't just go off to take care of it on my own. I don't want to do this on my own. Plus, you deserve revenge against him as much as I do. I know you're about doing things by the book. Alex was too. But this must end. Not just for me, or for you. For everyone that they've ever hurt and for everyone he's still planning on hurting. We don't know if he knows what has happened, so maybe it's our turn to get ahead of him. Somehow anyways."

"We'll figure it out. And if you do have a panic attack or anything, you can always come to me. You're not alone in this." Right then, the phone rang.

"Honey, it's for you." Iris came in handing Sam the phone.

"Thanks, honey." He took the phone and walked into the living room.

"Can I ask you something?"

"Sure."

"Adrianna," Iris sat down across from her. "Did you ever tell Alex about your panic attacks and nightmares?"

"No. I never told him about the letters either. I knew I would eventually, but I didn't plan on telling him about the nightmares and stuff. There wasn't really a reason to. But I ended up telling them both when they showed up in Luray."

"He loved you though. You could've talked to him about it. You know that."

"Yeah. I know. I just- we were just talking, you know? We weren't together. Y'all keep saying he loved me, but he barely knew me. We talked every day, but we never get to spend time together. Plus, my family just died a year ago. Isn't that bad if I had let myself be with Alex? I really like Alex. Liked Alex. But I wasn't ready to be in a relationship with him. And then he showed up. We had two days. And I let myself get close. Really close. Only to have him ripped away from me too. Now, his death is my fault too." She cried. A couple tears slid down her face and landed on the papers in front of her.

"Oh, honey. I didn't mean to get you going. I'm sorry. Look, of course you're feeling pulled all these different ways. Alex knew that. He even told us that he wanted to go really slow and not push you because you just lost your husband. And Alex dying was not your fault. From what I understand, he chose to save you. He wanted to protect you. He made that choice. And everything that has happened, that's the Stalker's doing. And his partner. Not yours. Do not beat yourself up over stuff like that. That's not on you."

She wiped her eyes and tried to force herself to calm down, taking a drink of her sweet tea. Sam walked back into the room, handing the phone to his wife. "That was the medical examiner. He said the test results came back but he can't identify who he is still. He's trying some more test and going to run past medical issues to see if anything pops up."

"Well shit." Iris said. "Can't catch a break, can you?" She looked down at the files and added. "Do you think the partner did any of the killing?"

"We don't know. Probably. Why?" Sam replied.

"It's simply weird. How can somebody be friends with someone like that? Especially if he knew what he did?"

"That's it!" Adrianna exclaimed.

"What is?" Sam asked, hurrying to sit back down.

"We have to focus on how they met. Find out how each victim came across the Stalker, and it should tell us more about where he goes and what he does. We get that- we can find out how he met his partner."

"That doesn't help you find him though, does it?" asked Iris.

"Actually… yeah it does. If we can find out how and where they met, we can at least find a picture of him someone on a security camera or something in that area. It could help us find out his name." they exchanged looks for a second. "Honey, do you mind if I use the wall again?"

She huffed and walked back through the doorway. "You didn't ask last time. Go ahead. I'll get to making some coffee."

Five

The next morning, Adrianna woke up on the couch before the Jones'. After folding the blankets and putting them in the basket in the corner of the room, she opened the living room curtains to let some light in. By the time she came out of the bathroom, Iris was already in the kitchen making coffee and breakfast.

"Good morning."

"Good morning. How did you sleep?"

"Like a rock." She laughed. After making her a cup, she thanked her for the coffee and sat down at the little kitchen table by the window. Watching the leaves float on the air outside, she sipped her coffee. The smell of strong coffee and hazelnut wafted up her nose, adding to the feel of fall. Hazelnut was Aunt Missy's favorite creamer. I can't believe I hadn't remembered that until now, she thought. Squirrels pranced and pounced playfully through the dry leaves, crunching them under their little feet.

Soon the smell of bacon and syrup interrupted her daydreaming. She turned around in her seat just in time to see Sam walk in the room, wearing old blue jeans and a tee-shirt. She smiled and giggled to herself a bit.

Hearing her giggle, he turned and asked, "What?"

"Nothing. I just have never seen you in regular clothes before. I mean, I know you and Alex wore button-ups and jeans as Detectives, but jeans and a tee-shirt is a little different."

"Oh. Well, I don't get to be super casual very often. Even when I'm off for the day, there's always a chance of getting called in on a case." He took a sip of coffee and helped the women bring the plates of food over to the table and continued. "Are you still up for today?"

"Yes." She answered somberly. "For Alex."

He nodded his head and sat down. "They're setting up the services for tomorrow." The women just nodded in understanding.

Adrianna took a bite of her bacon and pancakes. "These are great, Iris. Thank you."

"You're welcome."

They sat in silence for a long time. The only sound heard was the scraping of forks on their plates as they ate and drank. Even though it was a delicious meal, they all knew what was coming. Adrianna and Sam had stayed up until midnight, when Iris had then made Sam go to bed. Over most of the wall in the dining room was photographs, names, and a map of Staten Island. The map was dotted with all the abduction sites, crime scenes, and where each victim's body had been found. Photos of the warehouse was scattered along the table, while victim files were splayed on the table. They had spent so much time on setting it up after dinner, that the only thing they accomplished getting done was plotting on the map. They still had to find out how he found each victim and where they met the first time. Each one was too personal to him to be a random target.

The Adrianna Swift Series
Swift Snake

Once their bellies were full, Adrianna went to take a shower and get ready for the day. The meal weighed heavy on her stomach, but she knew Sam would never let her leave to go on a run. She'd have to do without, until she could go home. She washed mindlessly, only thinking of connecting the dots and finding the partner. After donning her clothes and putting away her things, she wandered into the living room where she could hear the Jones' talking. The sound of the television caught her attention as she entered the room.

"…the newest victim of the Staten Island Stalker case, a Staten Island detective, Alex Brenner. He died late Monday night, protecting another victim of the Staten Island Stalker, Katherine Davidson. You may remember her from a year ago, when she was found in a warehouse after the Stalker had murdered her husband and daughter. Now the location where this happened Monday, has not yet been given to us, but we have learned that the Staten Island Stalker is indeed dead. Yes, you heard that right folks. The Staten Island Stalker has been killed by none less than Ms. Davidson herself. No news yet of whether she will be charged. Tune in this evening at five for our…" Iris turned off the television.

"Adrianna…"

"So, has any charges been filed against me?"

"No." said Sam firmly, standing up. "And none will be. Don't listen to the television. The damn press always tries to twist everything around. You don't have anything to worry about."

"I'm not worried about that. If they really want to put me in jail, I'll go after we catch the partner. Not before. Otherwise I will disappear. But we have another problem."

"You noticed that too, huh?"

"Yeah. They just told everybody that the Stalker's dead. If his partner didn't know already, he does now. And he knows I'm the one who did it. He's going to be pissed. He could run and disappear, and we could never find him now."

"Yes. Or he could get pissed and try to get the attention in the media again. He could be driven to kill someone else now, so everyone fears them again. Or even to try to clear the Stalkers name completely."

"Either way, we just lost our advantage."

The Adrianna Swift Series
Swift Snake

Book 2
Written by N L Hiser

<u>Six</u>

An hour later, Adrianna and Sam pulled up to Alex's house. It was a small grey house with a tiny porch on the front, right on the outskirts of town. As they walked through the front door, a breeze blew through the downstairs grazing them as they entered. Silently glancing at each other, they quietly walked through the house, checking each room for someone that shouldn't be there.

After the last room was checked, Sam called, "It's clear."

"He just left his bedroom window cracked." She close and locked it. Suddenly, Adrianna heard a tiny meow come from the bathroom. She stepped around the door. "Aww. Hi there, pretty kitty. What's your name?"

Sam walked in behind her. "I didn't know he had a cat."

"Neither did I. He might not have told anyone because people still think cats are just for girls." She checked the tag on the cat collar. "Aww, well hello Tiger. That's a perfect name for you with your little stripes, isn't it?" Tiger meowed and rubbed against her hand. "Does Alex have any family that'll take him?"

"I doubt it. I've only met his parents once when they came in for the holidays one year. They don't strike me as the pet type if you catch my drift." He watched he pet Tiger for a minute and smiled. "Why don't you take him? We can take him and his things back to the house with us, and then you can take him with you after everything's over. I think Alex would've liked you to have him."

Thinking about it for a moment she asked, "Iris won't mind us bringing him back to the house?"

He laughed. "No. As long as he's not staying for good, she won't mind at all. We've had our share of cats and dogs. Fish too. But now that our kids are grown and have taken their pets with them, and ours have passed, we don't want any more pets. But she won't mind you bringing Tiger back with you at all. She'll probably want to spoil him actually."

Adrianna smiled. "Alright. What do you think, Tiger? You want to live with me?" Tiger meowed. "I guess I'll take that as a yes." She giggled. "Come on. Let's get you some food and gather your things."

"I'll be down in just a minute. I have to find Alex's uniform."

"Alright." Adrianna headed downstairs. She walked to the kitchen as Tiger followed close behind. "Come on, pretty boy."

She found the food and filled his bowl. Finding an empty box by the back door, she grabbed it and began to fill it with all the cat toys, treats, litter, and food. She went room to room and found his litter box by the laundry machine. Bringing that as well, she placed the then empty food bowl on top of the box and dropped everything by the front door. She was just putting Tiger into his carrier when Sam returned downstairs.

"Have you seen a desk anywhere?"

"It looks like he uses his kitchen table as one."

"Oh, okay. Help me search for a will?"

"Of course."

They searched the cluttered kitchen table for any important documents they may need for the funeral. "I haven't seen a will anywhere. Are you sure he had one?"

"Yes. We have one filed at headquarters at all times, but the chief said he had mentioned that he wanted to revise it. The chief said he thought he might have a draft of it here that they could still use, but if not, they'll just use the one they already have on file. We just wanted to make sure it was all set up exactly how he wanted."

"Oh. Well, maybe he has it hidden somewhere in his room. That's where I'd put it for safe keeping if I didn't have a safe. I'll go look really quick while you finish looking through these."

"Sounds good." He nodded barely lifting his eyes from the papers.

She quickly walked back upstairs, and into his bedroom. She looked in the top of his closet for it in a box but didn't find anything. Sitting down on the bed she asked, "Okay, if I was hiding my will, where would it I put it?"

Suddenly, a thought occurred to her. She stood up and looked under the mattress. Yes, she thought, and pulled out a manila envelope. She opened it and pulled out a couple pieces of paper. It was his newly, revised will, fully typed and signed just two weeks prior. Without bothering to read it, she put it back in the envelope and sealed it.

"I found it!" she yelled down the stairs. As she turned to leave the room, she noticed an old bracelet on the bedside table. Curious, she picked it up and twisted it in her fingers. The leather was worn and ragged, but except for a few nicks, the charm in the middle was shiny.

"I got that for him years ago, for Christmas." Said Sam, startling Adrianna. He smiled. "He always preferred a watch to looking at his phone."

She pressed the tiny button on the side of the charm, releasing the door for it to open. It revealed a sterling silver watch face and an engraving on the inside of the door that read, 'So You're Never Late Again'. She giggled.

"When he first joined the force here in Staten Island, he was always late in the morning when I'd pick him up. Wasn't ever much of a morning person. Here." He took the watch from her and put it around her wrist.

"I couldn't."

"Yes, you can. Besides, it'll give you something to remember us by when you leave."

"I could never forget you." She smiled as he clasped it closed. "Thank you."

"Come on. It's time we get back." He took the will she handed him and headed downstairs.

As soon as he was out of view, she took the sliver of paper from her pocket with 'Brenner' on it and placed it inside the watch before she closed it. Looking around the room where Alex used to live and sleep, she walked away downstairs. Meeting Sam by the door, she picked up Tiger and his things and followed Sam out into the cool air.

As they loaded the car, a cool breeze blew, sending fall leaves flying across the road and landing on the car. Tiger meowed and tried to pounce on a leaf that landed by his carrier. She bent over to pick him up, but stood up quickly, scaring him. "Shh." She whispered to him abruptly.

"What's wrong?" Sam asked, raising his eyebrow to her.

The little hairs on the back of her neck stood up, as heat rose in her back. She spun around, scanning the streets around them frantically. "Someone's watching us." She whispered.

"It could be someone that seen the news, Adrianna. We don't know for sure that he's even in Staten Island right now."

Still, the sense of unease wouldn't go away. She gently placed Tiger in the car, and sat down in the passenger seat, never ceasing to scan the areas around them. Sam looked down the streets too, but there was no one out. Not even neighbors. He locked the doors, trying to make Adrianna feel safe, put the car in gear and drove away. A few streets later, she started to calm down as her shoulders dropped and she took a deep, steadying breath.

"Are you okay?"

"Yes. I'm sorry. You're right, it could've just been someone that seen the news and was staring out of their window. But I felt them staring at us. Watching us. I've felt it every time the Stalker was close, even when I didn't find out he was following me until later. I know it may be ridiculous, but I need to trust my instincts."

"I get it. Besides, it's much better to be safe, than to be sorry. It's good you trust your instincts. Not many people do."

"I just wish I had learned to trust them before any of this happened. Maybe I would have noticed that I was being followed before he ever came into my house that night."

"Don't beat yourself up over it. Everyone gets caught off guard sometimes. Especially when you're busy with children."

"I know." She thought for a while as they passed through town. "Say he is here. Say he followed us back to town and knew what happened before the press did. What's he doing?"

"Well, even if he didn't follow us back and didn't find out until the news this morning, it's already noon. We expected to hear about something happening before now. What's he waiting for?"

"What if it's me, and he wants revenge?"

"If so, he still hasn't made a move. He must be planning something."

"We could bait him."

"What do you mean?"

"I could be the bait. As soon as we know he's watching, we could set a trap. Let him come for me and when he does, capture him."

"No!" he said sternly. "We are not using you as bait. That is the worst-case scenario. Understand?"

"Why?"

"Well for one, it's too dangerous. And for two, we don't even know what he looks like. It would be incredibly stupid to set a trap, not knowing what the bait even looks like. If we can't see him coming, we can't trap him."

The Adrianna Swift Series
Swift Snake

"Okay. So, what do we do?"

"We stick to the plan."

Book 2
Written by N L Hiser

<u>Seven</u>

They stopped by the store on the way back to the house, and Sam ran in to pick up some things on Iris's list, so Adrianna decided to sit in the car and wait with Tiger. Talking to him and petting him through his carrier, she tried to ignore the ping in her gut telling her that the partner was in Staten Island following them. He could be watching me now, she thought, glancing out of the window again. But the only people she saw were shoppers bustling in and out of the store. Maybe I am just being paranoid.

Then, a knock hit the back windshield, causing Adrianna and Tiger to jump in fright. Looking through the back she saw Sam motioning for her to pop the trunk. Laughing at herself, she popped the latch and resumed petting Tiger, trying to calm him back down.

"Did I scare you?" he laughed, getting in the car.

"You scared us both." She chuckled. "I thought it'd take you longer in there."

"Oh no. I hate shopping. I make it a point to get in and out as fast as I can." He smiled. "They stopped at the funeral home to quickly drop off Alex's uniform and give his will to the chief that had agreed to meet them there. A few short minutes later, they were back on the road.

Then Adrianna's phone vibrated in her pocket. She took it out and saw a text from Sara, 'OMG! I just seen the news. Call me ASAP!'

"Everything okay?"

"Yeah. The news is national now. My friend just texted me saying she just seen it and wants me to call her. I'll have to call her when we get back to the house, or she'll start calling and blowing up my phone. Plus, she likes to talk." She snickered.

"Trust me, I get it." He chuckled.

As they left the parking lot and headed to the house, she texted Sara and told her that she was on the way back to the house, but would call as soon as she got in. The ride back was a short five minutes long, but they were glad to be back. They unloaded the car and, after getting Tiger settled, Adrianna excused herself to call Sara.

She picked it up on the first ring. "Are you okay?"

She settled herself down on the couch and smiled. "Yes, I'm fine. I'm back in Staten Island with Jones. We brought the body-bodies back. Now, we're trying to find out who the partner is and catch him."

"What? What partner? Tell me everything!"

So, Adrianna told her all about how Alex and Sam came to tell her that the Stalker had escaped. She told her about how he showed on the first night, only to be zapped by the electric fence, and how he came back the next night. She told her everything. After she finished, she waited for Sara say something.

"So, how are you doing after all of this?"

"I'm…okay. I killed a man, and I don't feel bad about it. I sort of feel like a horrible person for it, but at the same time, I feel liberated. Plus, Alex. I feel so much about that, that I don't know how I feel anymore."

"That bastard deserved everything he got and more. We both know that. Hell, everyone does. Don't you dare try to make yourself feel bad about that. That was his doing. He decided to be a killer. Not you. As for Alex, honey, I know it's only been a year. But your husband isn't around anymore, and you do deserve to have a little joy in your life. So, don't for a second think that he would be upset with you over that or that you don't deserve to be happy. You do. I'm so sorry that you've lost him now too. But maybe he gave you a little happiness in the little while y'all had together?"

Adrianna smiled as color rose in her cheeks. "Yes. He did." She thought of how he held and made love to her mere hours before he was killed. They did get to spend two days together before he was gone.

"So? What happened?"

"In those two days, he showed me how much he really cared about me. He showed me what it was like to be touched and held by someone who genuinely cared for me. It had been so long since I felt that. My husband and I had been having issues before that night, so it kind of made it even more special, you know? And after the Stalker, I didn't know if I could ever stand for anyone to touch me again. Especially since I now have scars everywhere."

"Awe. Honey, that's amazing."

"Yeah, it was. But now he's been ripped away from me too."

"I know."

The women sat in silence for a while, just thinking about everything and quietly appreciating each other's company. "I think you need to change your mind set, Adrianna. Instead of him being ripped away from you too, maybe he was here in your life, at this point of your life, for a reason. Maybe you were in each other's lives for a reason, you know?"

"Maybe."

"So, now you're back in Staten Island, trying to find the partner and stop him? What are you going to do?"

"We have a few ideas."

"Well, let me hear it. Maybe you could use some fresh ears?"

She giggled, covering her mouth, and glancing around to make sure the Jones' hadn't heard her. She straightened herself and added, "You sure you want to know?"

"Absolutely. I'd do anything for you. You know that."

"Alright." She went on to tell Sara about their plan. Sara listened intently the entire time, only commenting here and there. Finally, at the end of it all, she took a long breath and stretched her back.

"Sounds like a good plan to me. How long is it going to take before you tell Jones you want to be the bait?"

"What? What do you mean?" she smiled.

"Oh, like I wasn't going to guess someone as hardheaded as you wouldn't want to offer herself up as bait to snag the killer. Ha! So, how long?"

"I-I asked him today." She murmured.

"Ha! I knew it. Ha-ha! And you tried to act like you had no idea what I was talking about."

"Alright, alright. Yes, I mentioned it and he said hell no. Can we move on now, please?" she huffed, shaking her head.

"Only if you promise me one thing."

"What's that?"

"When all of this is done and over with, and I come to hang out and spend the weekend or week or whatever, you have to tell me one thing about yourself that no one knows about."

"Okay. But why?"

"I don't know. Because I'm curious. There's still a lot I don't know about you." She laughed. "Promise?"

"I promise. Now, tell me what you've been up to lately."

Sara seemed pleased enough with the answer, so she went on to tell about her last few days. Adrianna found herself looking forward to seeing Sara after everything was over and done. She missed the spunky, redhead she had met, and

The Adrianna Swift Series
Swift Snake

couldn't wait to see her. After a couple hours or so, Iris came in to let her know that dinner was ready. She thanked her and sat up on the couch.

"I'll start getting everything packed, so as soon as you text me that you're ready to head my way, I'll be ready to go."

She beamed in excitement. "Awesome! I can't wait. I'm going to go get something to eat and get to working on this, but I'll text you tomorrow, alright?"

"Alright! Talk to you tomorrow. If you need me for anything, and I'm serious, you call me, okay?"

"Okay. Goodbye!"

"Bye!"

Eight

After dinner, Adrianna continued to work on the case. Iris continued to wash dishes in the kitchen as she had the previous night, while Sam was upstairs in the shower. She started writing a list of everything they needed to find out first, starting with tracking each of the victim's moments in the days leading up to their murders. The stalker always killed whatever family members were there that night, but it was always more of an after-thought. Something he did just to cover his tracks, and perhaps add to the torture of the women. If they could get the women's credit card information, ATM history, and maybe call history, they would be able to at least have an idea of where to look. Hopefully, at least.

She started to dig through the files of the victims, but no such information was written in them. The kitchen faucet turned off, and after a little bustling around, Iris joined Adrianna in the dining

room, fresh brewed coffee in tow. "Thank you."
She sighed, taking the mug.

Iris settled down in a chair with her coffee, smiling. "So?"

"So…?" the woman raised a brow at her as she took a gulp of her coffee.

"Who was that on the phone?"

"Oh." She chuckled. "I'm sorry I took so long on the phone. That was my friend, Sara. She's from Petersburg. I met her when I lived there for a little bit, before moving back home. She's great. One of those people that don't have a filter, and just say whatever they want and feel. I respect her a lot for that. You don't find that often anymore." She laughed, thinking of her friend. "It makes it easy to talk to her. She kind of forces it."

"That's great. Everyone needs a friend like that. Most especially you. It's got to be hard for you to trust people and open up. So, anyone that makes you feel secure and happy, you need that in your life. I'm glad you found her. Did you tell her about what's all going on?"

"Of course. She knows all of it. She gives me some good advice about it sometimes too. She gave me a lot of great ideas when I was setting up my house and property, too. She's good like that."

"She sounds like a smart girl. What does she do for a living?"

"She just got a job at the gym we had kickboxing class at. She's been going to school to teach yoga, self-defense, and kickboxing. She's one of the best I've ever seen. Definitely the best I've ever trained with. She's smaller than me, but she'll put a hurting on anyone that tries to hurt her. Unless it's a good-looking guy, anyways. She has a problem attracting assholes to her."

"Ha! That's a problem a lot of us women have. What did she think about you and Alex?"

"She loved every minute of it." She giggled. "She would've had us married by next Christmas if it was up to her."

Iris snorted coffee across the table. "I feel like I'd really like this Sara."

"You would. After everything's over, she's coming back to Luray with me and going to stay for a while. After we track down and stop the partner anyways." She sat back and took a drink of her coffee.

"You two will figure it out. The good guys always win. Do you want anything from the kitchen?" she asked, standing.

"No, thank you." She smiled. Iris went into the kitchen for some more coffee.

Sam came down the stairs and joined Adrianna in the dining room. "So, what's next?" Hearing her husband, Iris brought him a cup of coffee upon returning.

"We need access to the victim's personal records. ATM transaction history, card swipes, phone history. Anything that can tell us what they did in the days before their murders."

"That won't be easy now that I'm off the case and on leave for a few days. But I'll see what I can do."

"Thanks. Your buddies at the precinct probably already thought of it, so maybe it'll be easy to just get copies of it all. Either way, if anyone goes down, it's going to be me. Not you."

He chuckled. "We're partners in this. And neither of us are going down for anything. He is." He pointed to the picture on their board of the unknown partner, just a silhouette with a question mark. He took a drank of his coffee and made a quick phone call to someone he worked with. "Okay, they're looking into it. They're going to try to get back with me in the morning with what they've found. For now, all we can do is wait. And get some sleep tonight."

"Speaking of which, we'd like you to sleep in one of the spare bedrooms. No one sleeps in them now unless one of our kids come in to visit, so you have your pick of three. That way you can be more comfortable. And I think Tiger will enjoy being able to sleep in the room with you too." Iris added.

"Thank you. I really appreciate everything you both are doing for me. I'll never forget it."

"Like we said, you're family. You'll always have a place here." They both smiled as they drank, sitting down.

They all finished their drinks and headed upstairs to bed. She found herself looking back multiple times to make sure the doors were locked before they went upstairs. It was going to take a long time before she stopped looking over her shoulder. But at least there, with her gun close at hand, she felt safer than she would at a hotel. She knew she could trust the Jones'.

Nine

The street was hard and cold under her bare feet as she squinted into the blankets of fog around her. It was so thick she could barely see a foot in front of her. What sky she could see above her was dark, with few stars. The cold seeped into her skin, causing her to shiver; the moisture of the fog just made it worse. In nothing but her tee shirt and shorts pajamas, she stood freezing and alone, her heart racing.

"Hello?" she yelled into the fog. "Can anyone hear me?"

Psychotic laughter filled the air around her, pressing in on her ears and filling her head. Footsteps moved just outside of view, walking around her, encircling her. Her heart pounded in her chest as her breathing quickened.

Suddenly, the footsteps stopped, only a few feet behind her. Fear welled up inside her, screaming to her to run as she spun around. Another step sounded, and she ran in the opposite direction as quickly as she could. Running blind in the fog, she threw her arms up in front of her to try to protect herself. The steps picked up their pace and ran full speed toward her, their footsteps pounding the street like her heart pounded in her chest.

"No! Please! Leave me alone!" she screamed, running as fast as she could. The maniac's laughter again filled the air, but this time the footsteps stopped. She slowed to a stop and listened for them again.

After a long minute, the sound of running came at her from both sides. Bursting into a sprint, she ran as hard as she could. She whipped her head around to look behind her, but still saw nothing. Then, the laughter came again, this time followed by the sound of multiple sets of feet running at her. Every direction she turned; she could hear them coming at her.

Her eyes widened in terror. "Please! Stop! What do you want?"

Abruptly, she stepped on a hard piece of broken glass in the road and screamed in pain as she bled. She lost her footing and fell, landing hard on the ground. She cried as she tried to look around her to see who was after her. She sat crying, surrounded by the sound of running attackers, but still couldn't see anything except the thick, billowing fog. She sat with bated breath as a cold shiver ran down her spine when she saw a dark form approaching through the fog a moment later. With her eyes distracted, a hand slid out of the fog behind her and wrapped around her ankle. She realized too late, and screamed as she was pulled backward, and dragged along the ground. Dirt and mud covered her face and body, flying into her opened mouth as she screamed.

"No! Help!"

She jerked upright, swinging her arms and legs, trying to hit whoever had a hold of her. But, instead of connecting with an arm on her leg, she felt nothing. She looked around her and finds herself in her bed once again, tangled in her blankets. Tiger was standing alert and scared on the chair across the room watching her with wide eyes. "Oh my god." She whispers. "It's happening again."

She untangled herself from the blankets and slowly approached Tiger. "It's alright, Tiger. I just had a nightmare. I didn't mean to scare you." He

The Adrianna Swift Series
Swift Snake

meowed and came to her, his hair laying smoothly again as he rubbed against her offered hand. "Come on." She picked him up and scratched his head while she carried him gently to the bed. Crawling back in and setting Tiger on the bed in front of her, he laid down in her lap and rolled over for a belly scratch. "Good boy." She whispered.

She laid back against the pillows, letting her mind wander through her dream again, trying to remember the details. There was no face on the person who was chasing her. Taking a deep breath, she focused on her breathing and tried to relax and calm her still crazily beating heart.

Ten

Adrianna spent the rest of the night awake, paranoid that another nightmare would hit her. Worried she'd wake the Jones' if she left the room, she stayed in bed and played with Tiger. When her phone read five in the morning, she got up, stretched, and showered to start her day. Tiger spent the time on the sink, playing with one of his stuffed bird toys.

By the time she was out of the shower and dressed, she could hear the Jones' starting to move around a little in the other room. She scooped up Tiger and quietly walked out of the bedroom and down the hall towards the stairs, trying not to disturb Sam and Iris. Once downstairs, she went into the kitchen and brewed some coffee. She was already sitting down by the window, drinking her coffee when Iris walked in.

"Good morning."

"Good morning. How long have you been up?" Iris asked.

Lying, she answered, "Just an hour or so." She was careful to keep her eyes on Tiger playing in the floor. Tiger rolled over on his back and looked up at Adrianna, almost smiling as if to say, 'aren't I cute?' She grinned at him and leaned over to rub his belly.

Iris sat down across from her, sipped her coffee, and watched out the window. "It looks like it may rain today." She said, observing the grey clouds in the sky.

"My aunt used to say that if it rained during a funeral, it meant the angels were crying because they were calling one of their own home." She watched the storm clouds as they moved closer. The wind was high and fast, bringing the storm in faster as the minutes waned on.

"My Grandmama used to tell us that, too." Iris smiled. "Maybe it is true. I can't remember one day that there was a funeral I attended, where it hadn't rained."

"I can't either." She said quietly, furrowing her brows in deep thought. She reminisced on the day of her parent's funeral, and how the storm had lasted days. A thought occurring to her, she sat up and looked at Iris. "When are they burying the Stalker?"

"Oh, that won't be for a while. He's in cold storage until the case is solved or his name is known. Whichever comes first. Usually, the only exception is if the case goes cold. Then, they cremate the body, under John Doe and hold it in cold storage for evidence."

"Oh." She sat back, her shoulders slumping again. "Okay. As long as it's not today." Tiger hopped up into her lap and laid down. "Today is for Alex."

Iris smiled and nodded a silent agreement. "So, what would you like for breakfast?"

"I'm perfectly happy with anything. I'm not a picky person." She chuckled.

"I can make eggs, bacon, and biscuits. What do you think?"

"Sounds greats."

"Alright, then." She stood up and went over to the fridge to get everything out to start cooking breakfast.

Sam walked in a few minutes later as the women were talking about rainy days and the coming holidays. He made himself a cup of coffee and kissed his wife, before sitting down at the table. They talked about their kids and told Adrianna that they were all coming in for Christmas that year. They were incredibly excited, not only because they'd get to spend the holiday with all of their kids, but also their first grandbaby, a little boy named after Sam. He beamed, while he talked about baby Samuel.

Adrianna couldn't help but smile, as she listened to them talk. She hadn't ever heard Sam talk that much in one sitting, and their love for their children showed. Adrianna missed her daughter then, remembering Christmas morning opening presents, and how she had always got so excited for Santa Claus to come in the months leading up to Christmas. She missed Thanksgiving dinner and sharing what everyone was thankful for. A tear threatened to fall as she remembered her little girl saying during their last Thanksgiving dinner together, how she was thankful for having friends she could rely on and thankful for her family she loved so much. She may not have had a long life, Adrianna thought. But she was a good person, and I gave her everything I could during the time she was here.

"Are you alright, dear?" Iris asked, placing a plate in front of her and eyeing her closely.

"Huh? Oh. Yes, I'm alright. I was just remembering." She smiled.

"Remembering what?"

"The holidays the year before last, with my daughter and husband." She replied taking a bite of her eggs.

"Oh." Iris exchanged a sad look with Sam.

"It's alright, I promise. I enjoy hearing about your family. It helps me remember the good memories, instead of focusing on the bad."

"Are you positive?" asked Sam, concerned. She could see the sympathy in his eyes as he watched her.

The Adrianna Swift Series
Swift Snake

"Yes, I promise." She took another bite. "Do you think we'll get a lot of snow this year?"

"I don't know. We haven't gotten a lot the last few winters. I'd honestly like to see it snow nice, a few times, at least. Be a good white Christmas, like it was when we were growing up. It'd be nice to watch the neighbor's kids playing outside and building snowmen and having snowball fights. I miss hearing kids outside playing and having fun." Iris answered.

"I do too. I remember, when the kids were little, I'd get home from work and they'd be hiding outside and waiting for me. As soon as I'd get out of the cruiser, they'd pelt me with snowballs. They'd even get the neighbor's kids in on it somedays and I'd end up getting attacked by about ten kids all at once."

Iris giggled uncontrollably, the memory hitting her. "You never stood a chance!"

Sam laughed and shook his head. "They thought they were slick until I got them back. You remember the snowman incident?"

Iris burst out laughing, tears streaming down her face. "Oh my god, yes!"

"What's the snowman incident?" Adrianna asked curious.

"They had all made a snowman that day while I was at work. It stood taller than me, and pretty life like. Well, that night after the kids were all in bed asleep, I went outside to have a little fun of my own. I pushed the snowman a few feet closer to the house, and then I turned the head around like he was watching the house and moved his buttons and everything around."

"When they went outside the next morning, they all came running back in screaming that the snowman was alive!" Iris finished, screaming in laughter.

"It was hilarious!" Sam snickered. "I could hear them screaming from our bedroom. I couldn't let myself come downstairs until I could put on a straight face."

"Oh my god! I love it! Did they ever find out that you did it?"

The Adrianna Swift Series
Swift Snake

They exchanged a questioning look, before he answered. "I don't think they ever did." They giggled.

Adrianna laughed, picturing the kids' faces and imagining them telling their friends about the moving snowman. "I wish I had thought of something like that. The only prank I ever played on my daughter, was by accident. I got her one of those Elf On A Shelf dolls, but the first morning that she realized it had moved, she freaked out thinking it was going to come get her in her sleep." She chuckled remembering. "She was terrified of that thing."

Iris laughed. "Yeah our kids wouldn't have liked it either."

They continued their breakfast, while telling more stories about their kids. After everyone was done and the dishes cleaned and put away, they got ready and settled down in the living room, awaiting the time to go to Alex's funeral. After a few minutes, the phone rang. Sam walked out of the room, to answer the phone.

Coming back in a few minutes later, he looked at Adrianna and said, "They've got the information we requested last night. I'll get it while we're at the funeral."

Nodding, she turned on the television. There was sure to be something on the news about the case. Besides, it was best to know what the press got a hold of then, rather than later at the funeral. At first the news was on the weather, saying that a large storm was coming in from the north, bringing rain and colder weather with it. But then the news anchor continued to the headline news for the day. Alex's funeral.

"This isn't good. This means that the press will be packed in at the funeral." Sam responded angrily.

"It was going to happen anyways, honey. Especially when it's a cop. The only thing you can do is help to keep them controlled."

"I know, but this also makes it a target for the partner to show up, and we still have no clue who he is or what he looks like."

"It's alright, Sam. We'll keep an eye out. We can use it to our advantage. Have limited access, no press inside the perimeter, and photos taken of every guest."

"The chief will never go for it."

"We have to try. If he doesn't, we can still take photos ourselves. Of everyone we can. Just try not to be conspicuous. If we do it right, we could capture a photo of him, and compare it to past crime scene pictures and victim history. That could be a quick way to at least get a suspect list."

"Then, let's do it that way. The less people to know about it, the less chance of him realizing what we're doing. If he sees us setting him up, he could turn around and walk away, and disappear forever." Sam said, thinking.

"Then, that's what we'll do."

"Sounds good to me." Iris replied, holding onto her phone.

"Alright. Let's go." Said Adrianna. She stepped through the front door, and got hit by a huge gush of wind, almost knocking her backwards into the door. Steadying herself, she walked down the sidewalk, to the car. She held the door open against the wind, so Iris could get in without it hitting her. Hurrying, she slid into the backseat and closed the door behind her, as gently as she could so the wind wouldn't slam it.

Book 2
Written by N L Hiser

<u>Eleven</u>

T hey pulled into the funeral home a short while later, the silence in the car deafening. Sam turned off the engine and a fellow detective motioned for him to come over to the building. "You stay here. I'll be right back." He whispered. He opened the door and left the women in the car alone.

"It's going to be alright, Adrianna. Just keep your head. We can mourn our friend later, but we need to keep our heads, so we can find the partner. And because, well, Sam's really going to break down during this." Iris whispered.

"I know. We have to stay focused." She uttered back quietly, as much to herself as to Iris.

Sam walked back to the car a moment later, and opened the door for Iris, helping her out. Adrianna stepped out of the car behind her, being careful to keep her head down to shield her face with the church hat Iris lent her. Her eyes scanned the people around them from behind her sunglasses, thankful no one could see her watching.

She walked behind the Jones', never letting them out of sight. When asked, Sam introduced her as Adrianna, a long-time mutual friend of theirs and Alex's. Nobody seemed to question it, except the others from the station knew different, but went along with it. If the press found out who she was, it'd get crazy quick. Plus, it would be better if the partner didn't know she was there, unless he did follow them back to Staten Island. Then it would already be a big chance he was watching and following them. Adrianna remembered how Iris said that she looked so much different than her picture of before that night. Maybe it'd be enough to trick him too. She hoped at least.

They sat down in one of the front pews, with the rest of the uniforms in the pews behind them, and family on the opposite side. Adrianna fidgeted in her seat and repositioned the hat on her head. She went to take off her glasses, thinking it would be the respectful thing to do, when Iris leaned over and whispered in her ear.

"Leave them on. Women don't like to show their running makeup at funerals, that's why we wear the glasses."

"Hmm. I didn't know that." She whispered. "Thanks."

The preacher appeared through a door on the side of the room, and walked behind a small podium, to start the eulogy. The chief sat down beside Sam, and everyone grow silent.

The preacher spoke for a while and then they prayed. After the chief, Alex's father, and Sam went up to say a few words about Alex, a woman made her way over to the piano and started singing. Her voice mixed beautifully with the piano as she sang Sinatra's My Way.

Adrianna had always loved the song, but sang at a funeral, it hit you a little differently. Almost like instead of dying, Alex gave a magnificent performance, and then honorably bowed out of the world. She smiled as she realized it fit Alex perfectly. She could almost see Alex's boyish smile as he stood proudly in front of his funeral patrons. He would've liked it, she thought.

By the tune of the first chorus, everyone stood up and started walking up to see Alex off, one last time. Once the singer's voice quieted with the last note, Adrianna walked up to say her goodbyes. As she placed her hand on his, she leaned in close and whispered, "I will get the partner too, Alex. I promise." A single, large tear ran down her cheek and splashed onto his crisp collar. "Goodbye, Alex."

She turned and walked back over to the pew as Iris said her goodbyes. Adrianna seen Iris kiss her husband on the cheek and whisper something in his ear, before returning to Adrianna. Sam joined the Chief and fellow law enforcement as pallbearers for Alex. Adrianna and Iris walked outside and got into the car, ready to follow the convoy of cars to the resting plot. Soon the precession started to move forward. The Jones' car was only six or seven from the front, so they could see the front of the convoy easily as the rode down the little road. As they rounded a curve in the road, rain sprinkled down on the cars.

"Did you see anyone in the building?" Iris asked, quietly.

"No. Just his family and other law enforcement they work with. It's such a small room, they couldn't even fit half the people in that showed. We'll have to get photos at the plot. After everything is done, I'll let you two stay behind to say your final goodbyes and I'll head towards the car. That way I can try to sneak and get as many cars license plates and people leaving as I can. We just have to stay inconspicuous."

"Right." She replied, watching ahead.

"Is there a wake?"

"Ugh! Yes, but his parents only want immediate family attending. They actually made a point to tell the Chief that they don't even want guys he worked with, like Sam, to bother coming."

"That's fucked up. His family wasn't even around. He spent all his hours working. The force is his family. You two are his family. That's rude that they'd even go that far as to call the Chief. It's just fucked up."

"I know. But that also means, we only have this one chance to take photos, since we can't get any from the wake."

"True." She said as they came to a stop. Iris put the car in park, and quickly checked herself in the mirror before she opened the door.

"Let's door this." Adrianna whispered. Bracing herself, she opened her door and stepped out.

Thunder rumbled overhead as the sprinkles turned to large rain droplets. She quickly grabbed the umbrellas from the backseat and opened them for Iris and herself. They made their way over to the plot with the others, finding a spot up front to stand. After the casket was placed on the planks, Sam walked somberly back to his wife.

The preacher once again said a prayer and then the Chief came up to talk about Alex and his service to Staten Island and gave a signal to the men. Thunder rolled overhead again and a second later, the first volley of the twenty-one-gun salute erupted in the air around them. The tradition was over quickly and signaled the end of the funeral as the booms mixed with thunder above them.

As planned, Adrianna said her goodbyes first, placed a red rose on Alex's casket, and then hurried back to the cars. If anyone were paying attention, it would just appear like she was upset and trying to get to the car and out of the rain. Taking her phone out of her brassier quickly, she snapped as many photos of the cars and people around her as she dared and then stood by the car, to wait for the Jones'.

A strong gust of wind hit Adrianna from the side, catching the heavy umbrella, and almost blowing her over. Lightning cracked across the sky, followed by more thunder. It seemed the volume had been turned up. Wind blew again and her hat flew off her head and down to the ground. She hurriedly tried to pick it up when the wind caught it again and tore it away from her grasp.

"Shit!" she mumbled, only to be drowned out by the storm. She closed her umbrella and ran after the hat as it bounded on the ground and back into the air. After chasing it for a minute, she finally caught hold of it and held it to her chest. "Oh, thank goodness." She said, thinking of how upset Iris could have gotten if her hat was lost. She opened the umbrella as she looked around her, realizing how far away from the car she had ran. Seeing the head lights from the train of cars, she turned to head back.

Suddenly a hand shot out and grabbed her shoulder. Spinning around startled, her shoe slipped in the mud and she fell backwards, crashing down onto the ground. She jumped to her feet, staring at the man in front of her.

"I'm sorry. I didn't mean to frighten you. I just wanted to make sure you were alright. I saw you running." He smiled at her as he watched her intently. Something about his voice sent a shiver up Adrianna's spine.

"Who are you?" she kept her eyes on him, not trusting him for a second.

"My name's Scott. I'm a reporter for the Herald."

She relaxed slightly, realizing he was just another slimy journalist for the news. "Oh. Well, I'm fine, thank you. Just chasing my hat. The wind blew it away."

"It may have tried, but I don't think much of anything stands against you when you fight for something. Does it?" he replied, grinning. His long trench coat covered most of the black leather jacker and jeans he wore, not at all matching what she had seen other press guys wear. His greased back hair dripped from the rain as his dark brown eyes bore into hers, unsettling her.

"Maybe." She replied over the storm. "I need to go."

"I understand. You must be extremely busy lately." He snickered.

Adrianna backed away from him for a few steps, forcing herself to smile slightly so as not to be too obvious that she wanted away from him. As soon as she turned to head straight to the car, she lifted her phone up and tried to find him behind her in her camera. He had slightly turned from her, so she could only get one picture of him before she was too far away, and it was only of the side of his face. She couldn't really see a lot of details in it, but it'd have to do.

She continued to watch him in her camera for as long as she could, but the rain started to fall harder, making it difficult to see. When she got back to the car, the Jones' were there waiting for her. Getting in, they waited until the doors were closed and muted some of the sound outside to talk.

"Are you alright? When we got to the car and you weren't here, we started getting a little worried." Iris said.

"I'm fine. The wind blew your hat off my head, so I had to chase it. I did finally catch it, but it's a little muddy now though."

"Oh. Don't worry about that."

"When I finally caught it and turned to come back, a man surprised me, and I fell back in the mud. He said he was part of the press, but something about him creeped me out."

"Did he tell you his name?" asked Sam.

"Yeah, Scott. He said he worked for the Herald, but I'm not sure if he was telling the truth."

"I'll check into it and see if anyone by that name works there. If anything, we can get some background on him."

"Yeah." Adrianna replied quietly. Sam turned on the engine and they rode home. The entire way, she kept a picture of the man in her head and tried to remember everything he said to her. As soon as they got back, she'd right down as many details as she could.

Book 2
Written by N L Hiser

Twelve

That evening, **Adrianna and Sam spent** hours perusing through all the information they had gotten for the case and the photos from the funeral. They pin pointed location after location on the map, combed through list of numbers in the bank statements and phone records, and looked for any similarities. They couldn't find any likeness's anywhere, except a map of points surrounding the location of the warehouse. It was literally like the killer's central hub. Strings lined across many, connecting similar places certain victims may have shopped, like the grocery store on Clove Street. Looking over it all, she wasn't sure if it was going to help them much at all anymore.

They all decided they would rather have an easy dinner, so Adrianna ordered them some food. When the pizza delivery man arrived forty minutes later, she went to open the door. A young guy, likely still in high school, was standing at the door, holding a bag and a letter.

"Hi. I'm here with your pizza, but I found this on your doorstep here. Figured you didn't know it was out here, so I picked it up for you." He smiled.

"Oh, thank you. Yeah, with the rain out here, it probably wouldn't have lasted long." She laughed. She paid him for the pizza and told him to keep the change before she closed the door.

Taking the pizza to the dining room where Iris was bringing plates, she looked at the letter in her hand. On the front read one word: *Adrianna*. Putting the food down, she slowly opened the envelope, hesitant of what she might find. Inside was a letter, just like in the past, but this time written in a different handwriting. As she unfolded the letter, a small golden wedding band fell out onto the floor. She leaned over to pick it up and carefully examined it. Along the inside of the band was engraved, *Always and Forever Yours*.

Sam walked in from the bathroom and read the envelope on the table. Cursing, he took the ring from her. "This is evidence, Adrianna. Give me the letter."

Book 2
Written by N L Hiser

"After I read it." She said firmly, turning her back to him. After a moment, she turned back and said, "It's from the partner. It says, 'Katherine, I hope that pisses you off; me calling you Katherine. It isn't like you changed your name to hide from us, is it? Ha! Did you really think you'd get away with it? You killed him! We had such great plans for you, Katherine. And you ruined it! Completely ruined it! That's alright. He favored you for some stupid reason. I won't make the same mistake. Instead, I won't come for you first. Yeah. Instead, I've decided to send you a special gift. One that you should find…interesting. See you soon, Katherine.' It isn't signed with anything. Which, that would've made our job a little too easy, wouldn't it?" She handed the letter to Sam.

"Are you alright?" Iris asked her, coming to her side.

"Yes, but someone else isn't." She looked at the ring Sam was putting into a zip lock with the letter.

Book 2
Written by N L Hiser

Thirteen

The knowledge that he had another woman, and she was running out of time, if she wasn't already dead, kept spinning in Adrianna's mind as she laid in her bed. Tiger was curled up against her side, purring in his sleep. How are we going to find her before it's too late? She thought. I can't let him take another life. Not now. Not after we've come so far. I put an end to the Stalker, I need to stop his partner too. Before he kills someone else. I can't let him get away.

Sam had taken the envelope and the contents to the station, for evidence. Since he left a couple hours ago, a cruiser had been on patrol outside, supposedly to protect the house. Iris went around to check that all the windows and doors were locked after he left. They both thought that the partner would come back and try to break in to get the Adrianna.

They're wrong though, she had thought. He's not going to come back here. He's too smart for that. And he's not going to break in to get to me, she mused. He wants me to find her body. He wants me to blame myself for her dying. But I won't. He's making the choice to be what he is. Not me. But I will find him and stop him. Just like I did the Stalker.

She laid on the edge of the bed and thought about it for a long time. By the time she heard Sam come in the door downstairs, the moon was high behind the storm clouds. She stood up slowly, quietly walking to the window. She watched outside, scanning all the streets and sidewalks in view. The only person she saw out was a neighbor down the street, walking his dog in the yard. Most of the lights were out in the houses around her. She found herself hoping that everyone's houses were completely locked up, and hoping that the woman the partner had, was alive. I'm going to find you, she whispered.

The next morning, Adrianna got up and started working out. She knew Sam would never let her go out on a run since they knew that the partner was in Staten Island, so she decided to just do a minimal exercise in her room before taking a shower. While she did squats, pushups, crunches, and planks, she thought over her plan for the day.

By the time she was finished and got in the shower, the sun rose through the little window with a melody of birdsong, announcing the start of a beautiful day. "We're going to find her today." She told her reflection as she stood in front of the mirror. "We're going to find her."

She strolled into the kitchen minutes later, welcoming the smell of coffee that flooded her nostrils. Iris absentmindedly mumbled a good morning and continued cutting biscuits to put in the oven. Adrianna sat in silence for a while as she listened to the birds chirping and singing outside. Sam came in and sat down across from her, joining her as she watched out the window, deep in thought. There was a loud clank as Iris slid the baking sheet into the oven, startling her slightly. As Iris started to make gravy, Sam interrupted Adrianna's train of thought.

"I got some news this morning."

"What kind of news?"

"Well, bad news, but nothing we didn't already expect." He took another drink of coffee before clearing his throat and continuing. "They found the family this morning."

"How many?"

"Two DOA. The wife is missing as expected. We still don't have any leads on her whereabouts."

"How old was the kid?" she asked, hesitantly.

"See there's finally some good news. The two kids were at a sleepover a few streets over. The only ones found in the home were the husband and the wife's father. It seems he didn't realize the kids weren't there. Thankfully."

"That is good news. Sort of. What's going to happen to the kids?" she asked, her forehead furrowed in concern.

"Family has been contacted. Their aunt and uncle will be here to take care of them by tonight."

"That's good. How long does it look like she's been missing?"

"The medical examiner says the victims died at about one in the morning, yesterday. So, he's had her for over twenty-four hours now." Noticing her face lose its color, he continued carefully. "Adrianna, you're the only one on earth that truly knows what these two are capable of. Is there any chance she's still alive?"

She thought for a long moment, and then replied, "Honestly, if she has survived this long, it'd be a miracle. If she is alive, she won't last much longer. I don't remember ever seeing the partner while I was being-." She stopped, a shiver running down her back as she remembered. She cleared her throat and continued. "While he tortured me. So, I can't tell you if he even has a part in it. But if he's breaking into homes, killing, and kidnaping, we have to believe he'll go as far as the Stalker did. We can't underestimate him." She took a long drink from her coffee.

"Then we have to find her today. As soon as possible." Iris set their breakfast down on the table and took a seat next to Adrianna.

They ate quietly and with a determined speed. After they were finished, Iris told them she had to go to the store and run a few errands. Kissing her husband and smiling reassuringly at Adrianna, she left. Once he seen her drive off, he turned to Adrianna and said, "Let's get to work." She nodded and followed him to the dining room. She was ready to do whatever was needed to find and rescue the woman from the partner's grasp.

Fourteen

The partner watched as Iris left the house alone, leaving Adrianna with her husband. He sneered as Iris got into her car and drove away down the street. "Hmm... maybe somebody shouldn't stand between me and what I want." He murmured slyly.

He glanced back at the house as he turned the key and pulled the stolen car out onto the road. He followed Iris's red SUV, staying a few car lengths behind so as not to draw attention. Wright had taught him well. He knew everything he needed to know to keep from getting caught.

Being happily married with no kids living at home anymore made her an unusual target for them, something Wright never would have agreed to. The man sneered as he thought aloud. "Too bad you're not here to stop me this time." He laughed. He pulled his car into the parking lot behind Iris and parked as he watched her get out and walk into the store. "Besides, old pal, some things are just too sweet to pass by."

He watched as he came out a few minutes later and got in her car with her bags. A minute later, he followed her to another store just down the street. As she walked in, he glanced around at the crowded parking lot. "Not yet..." He whispered.

<u>Fifteen</u>

Adrianna and Sam immediately added the newest victims to the board, noting that it was the first that the partner performed alone, as far as they knew anyway. Then they went through each victim and made note of everywhere they had been in the days leading up to their demise. The only similarities they could find, was that they all seemed to shop at their nearest Stop and Shop's. There were multiple ones, but maybe they had gone there to pick their next target, she wondered. Suddenly, a thought occurred to her.

"Sam? Could you get the Stop and Shop's in these areas employment histories?"

"Yeah, but why? Almost all the victims went to different ones."

"Because I'm fairly sure they have employees that work at multiple areas, depending on where they're needed most. I know a few businesses that hire a handful of people for the same reason. Maybe our guys work at all of them, just going to whichever store the boss needs them at."

"Hmm. Yeah, that could be. We should check the security cameras at each one too. If they were scoping out new targets, maybe we can find them on one the cameras watching someone."

"True."

"Okay, let's go."

"Go? Aren't you going to ask one of your buddies at the station?"

"Nope. I can't stand sitting around all day. Plus, I'm not supposed to be on the case anyways, right? So, I can't keep calling the station to get them to do it. The chief's sure to find out. We can go do it ourselves. So, are you coming?" he asked, heading for the door. "Otherwise, I'll have an officer come sit outside."

Standing up, she followed him. "Yeah, okay." Tiger walked beside her, meowing for her attention. She pulled on her jacket and bent down. "I'll be back soon, Tiger. Don't be getting into trouble while I'm gone." She scratched behind his ears as he purred, and then walked outside with Sam, pulling the door shut behind her. Sam locked the door, they got in his car, and drove off down the road.

They arrived at the first store twenty minutes later. As soon as Sam put the car in park, he fixed his badge onto his belt and holstered his weapon to his hip. Adrianna watched, uncertain what she should do. Sensing her confusion, he turned the engine off and turned to her.

"Now, if anyone asks, you're doing a ride-along for an article. That way, you don't have to act any sort of way. Just follow my lead and don't ask too many questions and we'll be good to go."

"What if you get in trouble for working on the case?"

"I won't, so don't worry about that. Now, come on."

They got out of the car and strode into the store and walked straight to the register. A lanky young man stood behind the counter boredom etched on what part of his face you could see behind his too long bangs.

"Can I help you?" he asked, swinging his head jerkily, trying to see through his shaggy hair.

"Yes, I'm with the New York City Police Department. I'm Detective Jones, this is Megan. She is doing a ride-along today. Would your store happen to hire employees to work multiple locations?"

"No sir. Not this store. Our main store on Hylan Boulevard does the hiring."

"Have you had the main store send you an employee just for a day before? You know. Because you were short-handed."

"We used to get them all the time, but they actually sent us someone last month that's working here fulltime now. We haven't had a temporary employee in months."

"Alright. Well, thank you."

"No problem." The man replied, nonchalantly.

Sam turned and walked out of the door with Adrianna close behind.

"You didn't ask about the security cameras." She noted.

"I can't get those without a warrant. Besides, we need to track down exactly which stores had temporary employees first. Then we can get the security tapes from those stores around the time the victims were shopping there."

"Oh." Contemplating, she nodded and buckled her seat belt. "So…to Hylan?"

"Yep." The engine fired up and they pulled out of the parking lot.

It was another cool November day, but with virtually no clouds in the sky and the sun warming her skin through the window, it was perfect. It hadn't snowed in Staten Island yet, that year. It hadn't snowed anywhere yet. It seemed winter was holding back, rearing its freezing head to strike unexpectedly. Maybe it won't be a white Christmas this year, she thought. It never quite felt like Christmas on those years that the snow didn't come until around New Year's Day, but maybe that was a good thing. Maybe it'd be better if it didn't snow. Besides, she still needed to chop wood for the fireplace in Luray. Whenever she got back at least.

A car cut them off, causing Sam to hit the brakes so they wouldn't wreck. Sam just took it in stride, unbothered. The traffic was horrible, but it usually was. Adrianna always hated driving in it, and was thankful Sam was the one driving. Driving onto Hylan, she noticed a television playing in a restaurant through a window. Before it went out of view, the screen showed press standing outside the newest victim's home, police tape bordering the house.

A thought suddenly occurred to her and she blurted out, "What if they recognize me?"

"Who?"

"At the Stop and Shop."

"I doubt it."

"They're sharing more about the case on the news. If someone recognizes me asking questions, you'll get caught too."

"I'm not worried about getting caught. Yes, I'm not supposed to be working on the case. But Alex was my partner. Everyone I work with knows I'm not about to sit it out while they try to solve it themselves. They know I would still be looking into it myself. Now, if you get recognized, our biggest problem isn't going to be the chief. It's going to be the press. They'll try to say anything to cause problems because it's just more news to them. They don't care about other people's lives. If they get wind of you asking questions, they could say you have a vendetta. That, the Chief would have to silence quick. Even if it meant putting you in cuffs until everything's over."

"So, what are we going to do?"

"We have two options. Either I go in and ask alone, or…"

"Or what?"

"Or we change your face." Adrianna looked at him, frustration lining her face. Sam broke out into a bellowing chuckle. "I'm joking!" he laughed as he pulled into the Stop and Shop's lot. She sat smiling but considering her options. "I'll go in and question the boss. You sit here and relax, listen to music." He got out and walked in the store.

Adrianna sat in the car, not bothering to turn on the radio. "But you do have a good idea, Sam." She said aloud as she pondered.

The Adrianna Swift Series
Swift Snake

Almost twenty minutes later, Sam came outside with papers in his hand. As soon as he sat down in his seat, Adrianna asked him what happened.

"I got a short list of every temporary employee they have had on their payroll for the last two years. We'll have to compare them to the dates and stores each victim went to, but it's a start."

"Anything's better than nothing right now." She replied. She looked at the clock on the dash. "She's running out of time."

"I know. Let's get back to the house and compare those lists so we can get the camera footage."

"Right." She replied absently, as she read through the employee list. They rode in silence most of the way, until they stopped at a light a few streets over from the house. "Hey, did you ever hear about that guy from the funeral yesterday?"

"No…I haven't actually. I'll call and see if they got anything when we get inside."

"Okay."

Just before they reached their street, Sam got a call from Iris. He picked it up absentmindedly, as he pulled up to the house. Suddenly, his eyes widened in shock and fear. "What? Where?" Adrianna nudged him to see what was going on, and he ignored her. "Stay there. We're coming!" He whipped the car around abruptly, startling Adrianna as she held on to whatever she could. He hit the gas and they lurched forward and sped away.

"Sam! What's going on?" She yelled, frightened.

"Sorry, Adrianna. Iris's tires were slashed when she came out from the store and some guy decided to try to brandish a knife at her."

"Oh my god! Is she okay?"

"Yeah. She had her pistol, but as soon as she whipped it out, he ran away. Cops are there taking her statement."

"Holy shit. Sam, what if it was him? The partner."

"It may have been, but we don't know yet."

They sat in silence with bated breath as they rode to the store and to Iris. Fear and aner rose up within Adrianna as they got nearer. He could have gotten Iris too, she thought. What if he had killed her? That fucking bastard's not going to get away with this!

As they pulled up to the store parking lot, they could see two police cruisers parked behind Iris' car and Iris standing talking to the police lightheartedly. Sam jumped out and ran to her immediately as he put the car in park, Adrianna right at his heels. "Iris, are you okay?"

"Of course, honey." Iris smiled, welcoming his embrace. "The guy never touched me. As soon as I seen the knife, I drew my gun. He looked surprised and ran off. Got in a car and sped away."

"Thank goodness for that." Adrianna muttered, hugging her.

Sam thanked the officers and walked over to inspect the deflated and slashed tires. "Okay ladies. Let's get the bags in my car and I'll call to get it towed to the garage for new tires."

"Okay." They sighed. They loaded everything into the car and waited for the tow truck to arrive. They didn't talk, just sat, and waited. Thinking. After the car rolled away on the back of the tower, Sam put the car in gear and drove them home.

Once back, they brought everything inside and Sam excused himself to make a phone call. "He's worried." Iris whispered.

"Yeah." Adrianna sighed and smiled. "But at least you're home and alright. Let me help you put all this up."

"Oh, well thank you."

"Of course. Of, and before I forget, I need to ask you a favor. I thought about it earlier. I know this isn't the best time, but here lately it's never really been the best time for anything good."

"Anything dear." Iris smiled as they carried the bags to the kitchen.

"I'm going to get recognized when we're out. It could cause some issues, besides the fact that I don't want the press putting my name in any of it to begin with. Would you happen to know anyone who we could trust not to say anything, who could change my hair for me tomorrow? I'll tip her well for her silence, of course. I just don't know anyone that can keep quiet and I don't really know anyone around here anymore."

"Hmm, I'm sure I can think of someone." Iris smiled thoughtfully.

"Great! Thank you." She helped her put everything away and then headed to the dining room as Iris made tea.

She grabbed the paper Sam had placed on the table and started comparing dates with when the victims were at that store. As she skimmed over them all, she realized that six of the victims were at the stores when a temporary employee was working there. But knowing that the suspects were male, she could eliminate two of the instances immediately.

"That leaves these four." She muttered quietly to the room as she circled the names.

"Four what?" Sam asked from behind her, startling her. She turned to see him in the doorway as he walked over to take a seat in the chair beside her.

"Four potential suspects. As of right now, anyways."

"Hell, that's a smaller list than we usually start with." He laughed. "Let's see here…" He looked at the lists and said, "You can take off this one." He pointed. "He was working when I went in to get the employee records. He's in his late teens, early twenties. Too young to be our suspects. The rest, I'll run a background check on really quick and see what we can get from that."

"Okay, cool." She said, sitting back. "You know, I was thinking, do serial killers usually take souvenirs? I know it's in movies and television shows, but do they in real life?"

"Yeah, usually. It helps them connect and remember the crap they've done to people. Some of them even get excited when they look at them. Like they're reliving it or something. Why?"

"Did we ever find out what the souvenirs were that they took?"

"No. At first I thought it might be the wedding bands, since that's what the partner sent you. But you weren't missing yours, and after rechecking the other files, neither were the other victims. At least not in Staten Island. Though we don't have any reason to think they were anywhere else doing this." He noted.

"Hmm, so maybe the wedding bands are just the partner's thing?"

"Might be. You said you had never seen him during the time in the warehouse, right?"

"Right, but I was unconscious and barely able to see for most of the time I was there. I didn't see him in the house either, but he could've been downstairs waiting, just like he could've been at the warehouse."

"True. But I'm thinking, instead of doing the torture or the killing, maybe he likes to watch. We've ran across sickos that like to watch horrible stuff like that all the time. They could have everything recorded somewhere. Especially since they were following you for some time before that night, they could have recorded it. That could be their souvenir."

"Yeah. It could be. But the Stalker was vicious. I doubt he only had recordings."

"Probably not, but we have no clue what that is right now. And, if we're right about them recording everything, if we can find them all when we track the partner down, we can use it all as evidence. Not only in court, but to give the family's some closure. If anything, we'll be able to tell them why they chose their loved one."

Adrianna sat in thought for a moment. "How many people have they killed in Staten Island?"

"Including Alex," He hesitated. "and the woman that's missing and her family, sixteen."

"They wouldn't have just started by breaking into homes and killing people. And the torture? How could they have started with that? I mean, the only knowledge I have about serial killers, besides watching crime shows on the television, is what we've learned from this case. But doesn't it seem a bit extreme?"

"Yes, it does. But without the partner's fingerprints, we may never know what he's done. And the Stalker's aren't showing up in the system at all. Except on the past female victims he took. It's like he has never had a record anywhere." He said, frustration lining his face.

"But maybe we can track them another way, instead of fingerprints. The prints would speed up the process but…" Her voice trailed off as she continued with her thought.

"But…?"

"Maybe we can run facial recognition against the Stalker. Be able to find where he's been at least. We can look for him in the security footage from the Stop and Go's of course, but what if we got him on camera around the Island? And…maybe we can track both of them through their habits."

"What do you mean? Like if we find him on a camera at a restaurant, we can tell what he likes to eat?"

"Well yes and no. That can still be helpful later. But can we search other crimes with similarities to theirs? We know they like to break into people's homes, and that at least the Stalker likes to rape women. Can we see if there are unsolved rapes and break ins? Like I said, I don't know what y'all actually can research. I'm just thinking like a cop on a crime show." She laughed.

"Actually, yeah. That's a good idea. We'd have to go deeper than that though. Into everything they like. We'll go through every victim's report. If they were stabbed, burned, or beaten, that's a clue. We'll look for cases with each detail. I have to be honest; we will find a lot of cases and we might not be able to connect them to any of them. It could be a waste of time, but it could pay off."

"It'll be worth it. Anything to keep me busy and have possibly some good leads, will be worth the hassle. Just tell me what you need me to do."

"Well first things first." He said, straightening up. His eyes widened and filled with renewed eagerness and resolve. "Let's go through and find all the victim reports. We'll make a list of everything done to them. Anything that they put extra attention to, like more cutting than anything, take note of it. That could be important to them. The Stalker wore gloves for the most part but, if we can match the crimes to others, maybe he made a mistake somewhere."

"Or maybe the partner did. I hate to say it, but they're both very smart. To have gone so long and not be caught, and the fact that we had no clue there even was a partner until he texted the Stalker's phone after I killed him, they have to be smart."

"Yes, but we're smarter." Sam grinned. "Get started on the list. I'm going to go get some coffee brewing and call the station. See if we can get any type of facial recognition on him and see if we can get a warrant for the security footage at the Shop and Go's."

"Sounds good." She replied, grinning. She finally felt like they were getting somewhere, and she could tell by Sam's expression and sudden quickness to his step, that he was feeling it too.

<u>Sixteen</u>

S he gathered all the medical examiner's reports on the victims and started writing down everything that had been done to them. Sam returned to the room, talking on the phone, while she worked. She could smell the coffee as it brewed in the next room the strong aroma filled the dining room with a comforting fragrance.

As she wrote down electrocution on the list, she remembered the red-haired woman in the warehouse, and the handcuffs constraining her. Rubbing her wrists absently, she remembered how they hurt on her wrists and ankles as she fought them. Ankles! She thought. I didn't have cuffs on my ankles. What was it then?

She hurriedly wrote down 'hand-cuffed' and grabbed her file from the other side of the table. Going through the photos, she found one of her still on the table in the warehouse, just moments after the cops swarmed the place. She shook her head, trying to focus on the important details.

At the bottom of the photo, she seen two leather looking straps around her ankles, connected to the underside of the table. Writing down 'leather straps for ankles', not knowing how else to word it accurately, she closed her file and read through her list. All the things they had done to people. Innocent people. And to think, another woman was going through it right that moment.

The memory tugged at her heart as she sympathized with the woman she had never met. She knew what it felt like, what it took to endure it. She silently hoped that the partner was indeed, not into the torture part, and that maybe, just maybe, the woman was safe. Adrianna knew it would be a miracle if it were true, but all she could do was hope.

"Okay. Yeah, just let me know as soon as you can. Yeah. Thanks, Mike. I owe you one." Sam laughed as he talked. "Yeah, a few. I always do. Okay. Bye." He hung up the phone and sat at the table.

"Sorry about that. I can't sit while I talk on the phone. I always end up pacing."

She chuckled, "It doesn't bother me."

"He'll let us know when they get the security footage, and he said he'll look into the facial recognition idea. Nothing on the guy from the funeral. The Herald doesn't seem to have an employee by that name. Also, the autopsy just came back from the newest victims, the husband and father of the missing woman. Nothing new, but we did get the details. The husband was stabbed in the chest and the father's throat was slashed in his sleep. Still no news about the woman, Marian Smith. What do you have so far?"

"I wrote down everything the victims sustained from the attacks. Stabbing is already on the list, and so is cutting. But should slashing of the throat be on it too?"

"Oh, add it just in case."

"Alright." She said as she jotted it down quickly. "I also added hand cuffs and leather ankle straps. That's how I was bound in the warehouse. And the medical examiner's reports said the other women also had bruises and cuts from having their feet and hands bound. So, maybe they've done it before as well."

"Good point." He said, reading over the list. "You forgot stalking though. Even though we don't know how long they stalked the other victims, we know they stalked you over several states and sent you those letters."

"True." She agreed as he wrote it in. "Now, we need to add 'breaking and entering' to the list too."

"Got it." He agreed as well, adding it to the list. "Now, we compare this list with other crimes on the island and see if we can connect them to any others."

"Maybe we should look farther than just on Staten Island. They followed me to Virginia. For all we know, they were still hurting people after me. The Stalker was in prison for a year, but his partner wasn't."

"You're right. It's doubtful he was able to control his urges for the year. Plus, if you're right, they could have been doing this for a long time before we caught onto them. We'll need to expand the search, not only in different states, but also in the years before the attacks started happening on Staten Island." She nodded and suddenly felt sickened by what they may not have found yet.

Sam wrote a note on the bottom of the paper to his friend at the department, telling him to what to do. Then he walked into the office in the next room, to fax the paper to him. Adrianna stood up, stretched her back, and went into the kitchen to make a cup of coffee.

She poured some coffee into a mug over her sugar and creamer, stirring it slowly with a spoon. Taking a long drink, she smiled, feeling it warm her. Suddenly, a thud hit behind her, scaring her, and almost causing her to spew coffee everywhere. Spinning around, she seen Iris standing just on the other side of the doorway, eyes wide in fright.

"Oh my gosh!" Iris squeaked. "I'm so sorry. I thought you were still in the dining room with Sam and came for some coffee. I didn't mean to scare you. When I turned the corner and you were there, it about scared the daylights out of me and I dropped the laundry basket."

Adrianna grabbed the hand towel, laughing. She bent over to clean up the coffee she had spilled on the floor. "No, I'm sorry. I heard a thump behind me, and it made me jump." She giggled, tossing the towel into the empty sink. "I guess I'm just jumpy."

"You and me both, apparently." Iris laughed. "I haven't had a fright like that in years." She giggled, her hand over her heart.

Still shaking, Adrianna sat down at the little table with her coffee. A moment later, Iris sat down on the opposite chair with her fresh cup of coffee, still giggling. Adrianna chuckled as she steadied her hands and took a sip.

"What's going on?" Sam asked as he appeared through the doorway.

"Nothing." They said in unison, causing them to laugh harder.

"We just scared each other is all." Replied Iris, after catching her breath.

"Oh!" He chuckled. "So, that's what that noise was."

"Yep." Adrianna replied, smiling. "You sent it?"

"Yes, ma'am. He just texted me that he got it on his end, so now all we can do it wait."

"Ugh! That's the hardest part." Iris interjected.

"True, but it is what it is." Sam said, shrugging.

"Well, since you have to wait anyways," said Iris. "What would you two like to eat for dinner?"

Considering for a few moments, they all sipped their coffee. Sam leaned back against the refrigerator and answered, "How about some fried chicken?"

"Your doctor said you need to watch your cholesterol, honey. Maybe in a few days, but not tonight. You've already had fried chicken for lunch yesterday."

"Oh, alright." He whined.

Iris just shook her head and grinned. "What about you? What do you like?"

"I'm not picky." She countered, trying to avoid the question. She was already staying in their house, and with a new cat. She didn't want to be any more of a bother.

"You know she isn't going to let you off the hook that easy." Sam chuckled.

"Nope. Now come on. Tell me what your favorite meal is. Please. Seriously, it's no trouble."

"Okay. If you let me cook tonight. You've cooked for me every day I've been here. It's the least I can do."

"Well, I appreciate that, but it's not happening. I can't let you come here and having you cooking for us. You're our guest. And I enjoy cooking. Besides, I don't work anymore. I just keep up the house and do errands. The kids are all grown and out on their own. I like having you here, and I love to cook for people I care about. You just keep doing what you're doing. I'll take care of the cooking. Okay?"

Adrianna glanced over at Sam who only shrugged. He knew better than argue with his wife. Deciding to give in, she replied. "Alright."

"Good." Iris smiled. "Now, what would you like to eat?"

"Do y'all like spaghetti?" she asked.

"Sure do." Sam interjected.

"Then, that sounds great to me."

"Perfect! Spaghetti it is." Iris triumphantly grinned ear to ear.

"Thank you, Iris."

"Thank you, too, Adrianna."

She got up and refilled her coffee, before returning into the dining room. Sam came in seconds later with a mischievous grin upon his face. Deciding to stand awhile, Adrianna walked over to look at the map that was tacked onto the wall. He walked over and stood beside her, still grinning.

"What are you smiling about?" Her brow rose, questioningly.

"Spaghetti isn't your favorite meal, is it?" He uttered quietly, only loud enough for her to hear.

"Nope." She cracked a crooked grin. "But I do love it."

The Adrianna Swift Series
Swift Snake

"The pasta or winning?"

"Both." She whispered.

A small giggle escaped Sam's mouth as he turned his attention back to the case.

Book 2
Written by N L Hiser

<u>Seventeen</u>

T hey waited for the rest of the day, **but** never heard anything. Sam texted his friend, Mike, from the station, after Adrianna persisted to tell him that they were running out of time, but his friend never replied. Finally, it was time for dinner.

"Don't worry, Adrianna. We'll hear something soon." Sam reassured her as they sat down to eat.

Marian Smith was stilling missing, and if by some miracle she was still alive, they knew it wouldn't be for much longer. As the minutes passed to hours and the day turned to night, they grew increasingly anxious. Adrianna spun her spaghetti onto her fork, taking a bite. With her nerves overworked and knowing how many cups of coffee she had throughout the day, she knew she needed to eat. It was delicious and thanked Iris. She hoped Iris didn't catch the look on her face as she forced herself to eat. She tried to focus and not think of anything else, knowing she needed the fuel, but the helpless thoughts kept permeating her mind, ruining her appetite.

Suddenly, the phone rang in the kitchen, causing them all to jump in anticipation. Sam stood and went to answer the phone. Iris reached over the table and placed a hand on hers. Neither spoke. They just waited with bated breath and listened for Sam to speak. They could hear him pick up the phone and respond, "Jones residence."

After a quick, "Oh, hi! Yes, she's here. Just a second." He returned with the phone in hand. "It's your sister."

"Oh!" Iris hurriedly took the phone and walked into the hallway. Adrianna relaxed slightly and continued eating. Soon, Iris came back in and returned to her food.

"What was she all excited about?" Sam asked, curious and trying to divert their thoughts.

"Our niece just got engaged."

"Really? To that architect she's been dating?"

"Yep." Iris replied around a meatball.

"Well, that's great to hear. I'm glad she's happy. She's a good kid. They seemed really good together the last time we seen them."

"I agree. I liked him too. Seems like he treats her right and all."

"Good. Wouldn't want me to deal with him otherwise."

"Oh, Sam!" She laughed, almost spraying spaghetti across the table.

"What?" He asked, smiling incredulously as he stuck his chest out. "I'll put a whooping on him!"

Iris abrupted in a fit of uncontrollable laughter. Looking over at Adrianna, she explained. "A few years ago, our daughter decided to bring home a young guy that rode a motorcycle and was apparently, the struggling artist type. At least that's what he said he did for a living.

Come to find out, he was a college dropout that was in trouble for drinking and driving through a sorority building on his bike. Our daughter thought that made him cool and fell for him. Sam here thought it'd be a good idea to run the kid's background. Once he found out, him and Alex made him leave.

The last thing the guy said as he spun off on his bike was 'I only did it so I could see some naked chicks, but instead I got my ass kicked by a bunch of girls. It was hilarious!" she bellowed. "Sam and Alex were so mad at him, but then he said that and they both burst out laughing. Ever since then, when he talks about fighting somebody over the girls in the family, I instantly think of that day and can't help but laugh."

Adrianna giggled, imagining Alex's face after the guy rode off. Sam interjected saying, "So, now when I'm trying to be protective, she giggles."

"Yes, I do, Sam. But I know as well as any of our family and friends, you're the most loyal and dependable person in the world. You'd protect us from anyone trying to hurt us, and we know that. Besides, it was his fault it got stuck in my head." She chuckled, kissing her husband's cheek.

"Uh-hm. I'll show you something that'll get stuck in your head, woman." He played, whispering in her ear. She giggled uncontrollably, blushing a shade of rose.

Adrianna smiled at them and went back to her food. She finished eating and quickly put her dishes in the sink. Walking back, she poked her head in. Smiling as she seen Iris and Sam kissing, she decided not to interrupt them. Turning around, she headed upstairs to her room. As she neared the landing, Iris called after her.

"Adrianna?"

Turning around and craning her head so she could see her, she responded. "Yes?"

"Is everything alright?" Adrianna genuinely loved Iris. Her eyes were kind and sincere, no matter what she was talking about. Little lines were starting to etch her faces around her eyes and forehead, showing long years of stress, laughter, and sleepless nights.

"Yeah, everything's fine. I just can't wait. Never been particularly good with patience, well with my daughter being the only exception." She smiled to herself. "I'm just going to go take a shower and play with Tiger for a little bit. If you need me, just holler. And if you find out anything-."

"We'll let you know immediately." Iris interrupted.

"Thanks, Iris." She turned and went to her room.

Finally, inside and alone, she shut the door behind her, and leaned back against it. Taking a deep breath to calm herself so she wouldn't freak out, she slid down to sit on the floor as Tiger walked over to her.

"Hi, pretty boy. What have you been up to?" she said as she scratched his head.

He rubbed against her palm, begging for attention, and then promptly climbed up into her lap and laid down, rolling over to show her his belly. She giggled and rubbed his belly, inducing him to loud purrs. He stretched long and hard as she continued to rub his belly, and then as abruptly as he had laid down, he got up and walked away to curl up on the bed for a nap. Shaking her head at how cute he was, she stood up and stretched her tired back.

Walking over to her bags, she swiftly pulled out a pair of comfortable shorts and a tank top and changed. A moment later, she started her yoga and stretching. Tiger lifted his head from time to time to gawk at her, curiously trying to figure out what she was doing. Seemingly no longer interested, he laid his head on his paws and wrapped his tail around himself before dozing off. After she finished, she forced herself to sit quietly and try to meditate.

After two minutes, she gave up and headed to the bathroom for a long, hot shower. Turning the water on, she dropped her clothes on the floor and stepped behind the curtain. As the hot water steamed up the bathroom, her mind raced. Why haven't we heard anything, she wondered. It's been hours. And why the hell wasn't the guy answering Sam's texts?

Standing under the water, letting it warm her, she tried to drown out her thoughts. She leaned against the shower wall, feeling the cold of the tile against her as the hot water ran down her back. We have to find her before he kills her! There has to be something we can do! She thought, frustrated. She slowly sat down in the tub, letting the water rain down on her like a waterfall.

Trying to force herself to think of something else, anything else, she lathered up her loofah. Absently washing, she thought of her new house in Luray. The small cabin was picturesque. She could imagine what it'd look like once the snow hit. Perhaps, like a Thomas Kincaid painting, she thought fondly. After I put up some Christmas decorations and lights, it'll be beautiful. She could picture it perfectly. The Christmas tree would be in front of the living room window, lighted garland would wrap around the porch banisters, she'd hang a large old-fashioned wreath on the door, and a warm fire would crackle in the fireplace.

Suddenly her heart ached, as she remembered Alex laying on the ground behind the house. She had wanted to be with him and had wanted to invite him over for Christmas. Until they started getting close, she thought the holidays were going to be excruciatingly painful without her daughter and husband. But then, Alex came into the picture and changed her whole perspective. I was actually starting to look forward to Christmas, she thought. Tears filled her eyes and slid down her cheeks, blending with the water. Instead of fighting them, she let them fall. She knew she couldn't hold them back forever, but at least she was alone that time. Alone. The word brought a sickening feeling to her gut. I'm alone forever now, she cried.

She didn't come out of the bathroom until long after her fingers and toes wrinkled, and the water had started to grow cooler. Not wanting to use all the hot water, she immediately turned it off and dragged herself out and got dressed. She laid across her bed, not wanting to move, still fighting her racing mind.

She pulled her laptop closer to her and played some music. Turning the volume down so as not to disturb the Jones', she laid still and listened to her old favorites. Some brought even more tears when they reminded her of her family, but she didn't fight those tears either. Instead, she let them flow freely, relishing in the old memories even through the pain. Still, others reminded her of good times, like the songs she listened to in high school and in college with her best friends. Those were the ones that brought the quiet laughter as she was reminded of all the crazy things her and her friends had done back then.

She remembered her best friend and how she had stayed the night with her and helped when the guy she was dating cheated on her. Thinking of it after all that had happened in her life since then, she realized how silly worrying about him then was. But that's part of life, I guess, she thought. How some things can seem so trivial and heartbreaking, but then you look back and realize the person who was putting you through it, wasn't worth the time or effort. Just one of life's lessons I needed to learn, I guess.

She laid there in bed listening to music and rolling through her emotions and didn't want to get up. After a long while, she looked at the time, only to realize that she'd been upstairs for two hours. She turned off her music, rolled over to pet Tiger and grabbed her phone that he had decided to sleep on. It's a good thing I didn't get a call or anything, she giggled as she imagined him jumping up when it would've scared him.

"Alright," she whispered to herself. "I better go downstairs before they come up worrying."

Eighteen

A minute later, Adrianna found Iris and Sam in the living room watching the news. It was the same reporter as before, only this time he was talking about the missing woman.

"Hey, Adrianna. Are you okay? I was wondering when you were going to come down." Iris asked.

"I just assumed you fell asleep." Sam chuckled.

"I did." She said lightly as she sat down in the armchair. "I couldn't stop myself from thinking about the case, so I did some yoga and took a shower. Afterwards, I ended up sitting on the bed playing with Tiger and he fell asleep on my lap. I didn't have the heart to move him right away, so I just listened to some music for a little bit. I ended up waking up a few minutes ago, with Tiger sprawled out on top of me." She forced a small giggle, only lying a little bit.

"Oh. Are you sure you're okay? You look like you've been crying?" Iris pressed her.

Shaking her head, she replied. "I'm fine. It must be from just waking up. I didn't mean to fall asleep."

Iris laughed, "Well after eating and then doing yoga and a shower, I don't blame you. I'd probably still be asleep."

"Yeah, usually I just need to eat a good meal and I'm ready for a nap." Sam added chuckling. "Plus, we've been working all day. Staring at those papers all day will make you tired too, trust me."

"True." She commented. "What have you been up to?"

"Not much. Just been sitting here watching tv. We were talking about watching a movie. Want to watch one with us?" Iris asked.

"Sure. Why not?"

"What sort of movies do you like to watch?"

"A bit of everything." She answered. "Just not a lot of horror anymore."

"Oh, good. Because I don't really like scary movies." Iris commented.

Sam laughed and kissed his wife. "Maybe not, but I do like scaring you." He teased, grabbing her.

"Oh, stop it!" Iris squealed as she smacked his hands away.

Adrianna giggled at the sight of them. Finally, Sam let her go. Taking the remote from him, she refocused on the tv. "So, what do you all want to want?" she asked.

"Doesn't matter to me. Pick something you like. Like I said, I like a bit of everything, so I'll like it no matter what you choose."

"That's easy enough." Sam countered. "You want to make some popcorn while we pick out something. It'll take Iris a while to decide."

"Absolutely." Adrianna replied, walking to the kitchen. She found the bags of popcorn easily enough and put one in the microwave to pop. She could still hear them in the living room picking at each other, as they tried to decide what they wanted to watch. It made her happy to hear them being so loving toward one another.

Even though she loved her husband, her and Rick had been having issues for a year or more before that night. She couldn't understand it. It seemed they just stopped playing and teasing one another. They stopped loving on one another and never cuddled anymore. Instead, they had started to act less like a couple and more like roommates. He even stopped kissing her for no reason like he had before.

Adrianna had chalked it up to it being a 'midlife crisis' type of thing, but she couldn't help but feel like she had done something to turn him away. What if I let him down somehow? She thought. What would he think now? Humph! He'd probably tell me that I shouldn't be getting involved. That it was the cop's business and I need to stay out of it. Ugh! And he probably would've been right. The only thing is, I'm not that type of woman, she thought stubbornly.

The microwave beeped, startling her out of her reverie. Taking the bag out, she placed another in and started the timer again. She dumped the bag into a bowl she found in the cabinet and waited for the next to finish popping. When it was done, she poured a little more into the bowl and took both to the living room. As soon as she gave them the bowl and got ready, Iris pushed play.

They sat and watched a comedic movie about two friends traveling to interview a dictator. The FBI found out and asked them to assassinate the dictator for them, and it all went horribly and hysterically wrong. About halfway through the movie, Tiger strode in and leapt up onto Adrianna's lap, demanding attention. She absently petted him as they watched the movie.

By the time the movie ended, the night was late, so she placed her bag in the garbage and told them goodnight. Walking back upstairs, carrying a lazy kitty, she welcomed the sight of the bed as she closed her door behind her. Changing quickly, she gave Tiger a few treats and crawled into bed. Sleep took hold so fast that she didn't even know she was already dreaming.

Book 2
Written by N L Hiser

Nineteen

Throughout the wind blew hard outside, swinging one of the tree's branches into the window with a loud thud. The tree's tallest limbs were higher than the house, so she worried that the wind might blow it over onto the house as the Jones' slept. Tiger was no longer asleep on the bed, undoubtfully frightened by the bang on the window. She sat in the bed as she listened to the howling of the wind. Should I wake up Sam or should I wait until it gets worse? She wondered. I don't want it to damage their house.

Lightning struck with an ear shattering crack, lighting up the room. Thunder followed a moment later, rumbling so loud she thought she could feel it shake the earth. Rain pelted the windows and roof, pouring harder and harder until it was no longer possible to see out the window with any clarity. Lightning struck, once again illuminating the room, and hen in that instant flash, Adrianna realized the bedroom door was open.

The Adrianna Swift Series
Swift Snake

Certain that she had shut it, she slowly slid to the side of the bed and stood. She glanced at her bag, tempted to grab her gun, but didn't want to risk accidently shooting Sam or Iris. Plus, they didn't know she had brought it.

"Hello?" She asked quietly, staring at the open door. Too quietly for the storm raged over her voice. Straightening, again she asked, but louder. "Hello? Is anyone there?" There was no answer. She walked stealthily to the door. She listened closely, trying to hear anything around the storm raging outside. Seeing nothing on the left of the door, she pressed herself against the wall on the other side. She slowly edged herself to the door frame and prepared herself for what she'd see on the other side.

Lightning struck again outside, lighting the doorway. Taking advantage, she lunged around the door, fists up and ready. A large figure stood in front of her, silhouetted against the light behind it, coming through the window at the far end of the hall.

"Adrianna?" Sam shouted over the storm.

"Sam?"

"Oh, thank god!" Iris shouted, now coming out of their bedroom holding a flashlight.

"The storm knocked the power out. We heard you shout 'hello' and worried something was wrong." Sam said as they came closer, so they could hear each other.

"I'm okay. But I thought someone was in the house. The bedroom door was open when I woke up. Did you open the door?" She asked them.

They exchanged glances and shook their heads. "No, honey. We didn't open your door. Are you positive you didn't close it?"

"I'm positive. I make sure the doors are closed now. Extra bit of time to defend myself if I need to." She shrugged. "So, unless Tiger learned how to open doors, someone else is in this house."

"You two stay here. I'll go check it out." Sam shouted over the thunder.

"Hell no. You're not going without me and it's not safe up here either unless you checked each inch of it." She shook her head determined. Iris nodded in agreement.

"Fine. Stick right behind me and do what I say."

"Are there any weapons in the house?"

"Only my sidearm. Iris' is in the bedroom, but I'd rather not have another gun in this. We can grab something else on the way if we need to."

"Okay." They said. Adrianna grabbed Iris's arm and followed close behind Sam. She could feel her arm shaking uncontrollably in hers, and squeezed it gently, trying to reassure her. If anything happens to them, she thought, I don't know what I'll do.

They inched their way downstairs, one step at a time. She found herself thankful that the storm concealed their noisy movements but also wishing it were quiet, so she could hear if anyone were downstairs. Anxious and ready for a fight, she kept hold of Iris and made sure they stayed within an arms-length from Sam.

Moving room to room, they made sure no one was inside. As they entered each new room, Adrianna made sure to check in the closets and any hiding spots while Sam continued through. As they cleared the last area, concern reentered her mind. Sam and Iris seemed relieved and assured that it was safe, but Adrianna felt the familiar nagging pings in her gut. She walked to the back door and rechecked the lock, then looked out the window to the back porch. Seeing nothing unusual, she looked back at Sam and Iris.

"We need to make sure all the windows are locked." Knowing she wasn't ready to accept it was safe, they both nodded in agreement and went to check. "I'll check the ones in the living room and the front of the house." She said, heading back to the living room.

She checked all the windows, happy that they were all shut and locked. Coming to the last window, looking out into the yard from the living room, she noticed something just out of view on the porch, just outside the window. A sinking feeling filled her heart, afraid of what it might be. Going to the door, she peeked through the peephole but was unable to see anything. Finding it unlocked and the door not completely closed, she slowly grabbed the knob. Taking a steadying breath as she prepared herself for a fight, she whipped open the door.

"Sam!" she screamed. Laying on the door stoop splayed the missing woman, naked and bloody. Her eyes and mouth were wide open, not moving. She quickly checked her for a pulse, knowing in her heart she was already dead. Feeling no pulse, she focused on looking around her. She could barely see through the rain and the wind but didn't notice anything abnormal.

Sam appeared at her side, instantly realizing what was wrong and pulled Adrianna back into the house, locking the door immediately. He ran to Iris and told her to go sit down and no matter what, not to look outside. Then he turned and told Adrianna not to open the door for anyone and to keep Iris away from it. He then ran upstairs to get his cell phone.

"What's going on?" Iris asked, fear in her eyes.

Walking over to the couch, but refusing to sit, she replied. "The partner just delivered the missing woman to us."

"Delivered? What do you-?" Her eyes widen in fear as realization dawned on her. "Oh my god." She uttered.

Sam returned downstairs, talking into his phone rapidly. "…on my doorstep. Yeah, we think he may have come in the house, but we searched everywhere and didn't find anything."

"The front door was unlocked." Adrianna interrupted him.

"Shit! Yeah, she said the door was unlocked. Okay, just get here quick." He ended his call. "They're on their way."

"Who?" asked Iris.

"Everybody." Sam replied. "Adrianna, if the door was unlocked, why did you open it?"

"I saw something out of the corner of the window. I could tell something was on the stoop but couldn't tell what. Then I realized the door was unlocked."

"But why would you open it? You put yourself in danger."

"I've been in plenty of danger when he and his partner targeted me and my family over a year ago. I was ready for whatever was going to happen when I opened that door. Even if he were standing there, himself, I would die before I let him in here to hurt either one on you. I wouldn't let that happen. You know that."

He took a deep breath. "I know. I'm sorry. It's just if anything had happened to either of you-."

"But it didn't." said Iris, joining her husband and hugging him. "And we're safe. All of us."

He smiled at her, thankful for her constant reassurance. "I love you." He kissed her forehead protectively.

"I love you too, honey." Resting her head on his chest. After a few moments, she turned to Adrianna, unwilling to let go of her husband. "Are *you* alright?"

Her mind distracted, she realized Iris was talking to her. "Huh? Sorry, what did you say?"

"Are you alright?"

"Oh, yeah. I'm fine."

"Are you sure?" asked Sam, looking seriously concerned.

"Yeah. Why?"

"You saw her. Without warning. And you've been so focused on finding her before it was too late." He gently added.

"I know. But I'm alright. Really. It's not the worst I've ever seen. Though that was pretty bad…" she answered, her gaze going toward the door. "I know we've tried so hard to find her before time ran out, but he wasn't the stalker. We had no clue what he was going to do with her. For all we knew, he killed her immediately. We all knew her time was limited."

"True."

"Shouldn't we cover her or something? Since it's storming outside, can't that destroy any evidence?"

"We can't. Whatever we use will contaminate the body and any evidence. Besides, she's on the stoop, so she's protected by the porch roof. At least somewhat. We have to leave her as she is until the forensics team and medical examiner get here."

"I checked for a pulse. I knew by looking at her that she looked-. Well, I had to make sure. I pretty much looked dead when you all found me in that warehouse."

"Yeah, true. We always need to check, just in case. It's amazing what a person can go through."

"Yeah." She said quietly, inaudible over the storm. She watched out the window as the rain continued to pour down and listened to the thunder rumble and lightning strike. She watched for the emergency lights they knew were on their way to them. They just had to stay inside and safe, until they got there.

"Sam?" she asked, still looking out the window. "If he put her outside on the front porch, why did he unlock the door and come in? Why did he open my bedroom door? There was no rain or mud tracked anywhere in the house. Does that mean he came before the storm started? If he was in the house, what did he do inside?"

Sam watched Adrianna as she stared out of the window, unmoving. She stood rigid, each muscle alert and ready to be triggered. It reminded him of watching tigers on the television stalking its prey, waiting for it to come into reach. He had seen her once before with the same look; the moment after Alex was shot. She was not the timid and defenseless woman she seemed to be when he first met her, and he regretted doubting her.

He held Iris a little tighter, now slightly paranoid of what might lurk in the shadows just out of sight.

Book 2
Written by N L Hiser

Twenty

He crouched behind the parked car on the other side of the street, watching Adrianna through the living room window. He couldn't see her very clearly, even with his binoculars. But he could see enough.

He sneered and pushed his hair back out of his face. "I hope you like my gift." He laughed. "See you soon, *Katherine*." He put his binoculars in his leather jacket pocket and turned his back to the car, leaning against it.

The rain poured down on him, but he enjoyed it. Most people would say it was too cold, but his heart was as cold and sharp as a glacier. At least that's what he always told everyone. He could hear sirens wailing as they drew nearer. Turning slightly, he looked to see which way they were coming from. Seeing the first glares of lights on other vehicles to his left, he stood and placed an envelope under the windshield wiper of the car and speedily walked away from the sirens and lights. Once he was a few houses down the road, he dodged through a yard and out the back into another street.

Laughing manically now, he briskly walked over four more streets and down the sidewalk. Stopping at a black, extended cab truck with tented windows, he opened the door and climbed in. Turning the key in the ignition, he drove away into the dark and foul night.

Twenty-One

Adrianna finally relaxed slightly when she could see the first glaring lights of the emergency vehicles heading their way. As they neared, she could hear their sirens blare through the storm. They flooded the street a minute later, blocking off both ends.

Uniformed officers jumped and immediately sectioned off the area with yellow crime scene tape. The chief, along with a few other people with Forensics Unit on their vests came to the front door. Then the Medical Examiner truck pulled in, and after a moment the occupants started walking up to the front door as well.

Sam asked Iris to go to the back door and let in the Chief and his guys as soon as they came around. She nodded and kissed him on the cheek, before exiting the room. He double-checked that she was out of the room and quickly glanced at Adrianna before then unlocking and opening the front door. A blast of air flew through the door, followed by the deafening sound of the storm and the voices of everyone just outside.

"Jones, good. Are you all alright?" the Chief asked.

"Yes sir."

"Good. I'm glad. Any sign of the suspect?"

"No sir. But I would like to know how he got inside the house."

"We'll see what we can find out." He continued talking to the Medical Examiner and the forensics team. "Alright, you three follow me." He said motioning. They walked around the side of the house to the backdoor.

Adrianna could hear them talking in the kitchen and Iris offering to make coffee. She heard them tell her thank you and then heard their steps coming toward them. Out of nowhere, she felt something brush against her leg, startling her and causing her to jump. Looking down, she saw Tiger look up at her.

"Tiger! Oh my god. I'm so glad you're okay. I couldn't find you anywhere!" she sat down in the floor and picked him up to pull him in close. Wet fur clung to her skin and clothes. "Why are you wet?" she asked, worried. Checking him closely and relieved he wasn't bleeding, she said, "Was you outside in the rain?" He meowed quietly. "Poor thing." She wrapped him in her arms and tried to warm him.

"Who's this?" the Chief asked as he walked over to her.

"This is Tiger. He was Alex's cat."

"Alex? I didn't know he had a cat."

"Apparently no one did. We found him when we went to his place for his uniform and will. I'm going to take care of him now and take him back home with me after everything's over."

The older man smiled. "I think he would've liked that. And from the looks of it, so does Tiger."

"I guess when the bastard opened the doors, he let him outside. Now he's soaked, but at least he's safe."

"Yeah, he'll be alright. Jones said that the suspect opened your bedroom door?"

"Yeah. When I woke up, it was open. And the front door was unlocked. I don't get it. If he got in, and even made it in my room while I was sleeping, why didn't he do anything? I mean, what was the point of him coming in at all, if he wasn't going to try to kill me or anything, and he was just going to drop a body on the doorstep?"

He sat down on the armchair in front of her. "I really don't know, but we're going to try to find out. Now, how are you doing with all of this?"

"I'm fine. I just want to stop the bastard before he hurts anyone else. They've already destroyed so many lives."

Nodding in agreement, he continued. "You know he dropped the body here to intimidate you, right? I mean, the letter with the ring inside, practically taunting you. He's trying to put her death on you."

Adrianna searched his expression, knowing he was testing her just as much as warning her. "I know. But he's the one that killed her, not me. That bastard dug his own grave. I was done being intimidated when I knew the Stalker broke out of prison." She caressed the cat for a moment, contemplating. Standing up, still holding Tiger, she continued. "What do you need me to do?"

A small grin creased his mouth. "For now, take these two upstairs with you." He motioned. "That way you can get a towel to dry off your cat and they can search your room. We don't know what his reason was for going in your room, so maybe he left something behind. Or it could be him just trying to scare you with the fact that he was in there while you were asleep and defenseless. Either way, we need to make sure."

"Alright," she paused. "but let me make myself clear. I know you're in charge here, but you're not going to keep me out of the loop on this. He's after me, and he'll hurt who knows how many people until he either kills me or is stopped. And I will stop him. One way or another." She said and then walked away. Before she reached the stairs, she turned around and said, "and if he thought I was defenseless because I was asleep, he's wrong. I know how to defend myself now, and I won't go down without a fight again."

"Ma'am, I don't doubt that for a second." The Chief replied across the room.

The two men followed Adrianna to her room. Once inside, she left them to do what they needed too while she towel-dried Tiger. He didn't like it much, but he didn't try to claw her while she did it. After he was as dry as she could get him, she put him in his carrier and locked the door to make sure he didn't get out of the house while the doors were open downstairs.

"Do what you need to do. Just don't mess with my cat." She said, heading toward the door.

"Yes ma'am." They said as she disappeared through the door and headed downstairs.

The entire house was a buzz when she got downstairs. The storm had eased up a bit outside, so the noise from outside wasn't as loud. She made a beeline toward the kitchen, planning on getting a cup of coffee before anything else. As she neared the kitchen, Sam's voice rang out. Poking her head into the dining room where she heard him at, she seen him sitting with the Chief and surrounded by men talking on phones and looking at their papers.

"Uh, just a second, Sam. I need coffee. Want any?"

"Yes, please. But then come in here. We got a lot of work ahead of us."

"Copy that. I'll be just a second." She hurried through to the kitchen. Iris was busy making breakfast. "Why are you cooking? You could be in bed asleep. It's still super early."

"Ha! I can't sleep with all this going on." She laughed. "Besides, you all need to eat. My as well make myself useful."

"Well, thank you Iris. I have to grab coffee and meet Sam and the Chief in the dining room."

"Good. I'll brew another pot in just a minute."

Smiling she poured her and Sam a couple cups and added their preferred cream and sugar. "If you need anything, Iris, just come find me. Okay?"

"You too!" she smiled as Adrianna headed to the dining room.

Book 2
Written by N L Hiser

<u>Twenty-Two</u>

A

drianna!" Sam motioned for her to come sit next to him and the Chief. "Thank you. I was really wanting some coffee but hadn't made it there yet."

She laughed. "You know Iris is in there cooking for this army, don't you?" she said as she sat down. The coffee went down smooth. "Mm, perfect cup." She breathed.

"Of course, she is. Do you think she'd ever let people come over at two in the morning and not get everybody some food and coffee?"

"Yeah, not really." She laughed. She seen one of the men on the other side of the room eyeing her coffee. "She's brewing another pot right now. It should be ready in just a minute." She said to the man. He kindly said thanks and left the room, heading for the living room.

Just then the guys from upstairs walked in. "Sir, we found nothing. Not even a print."

"What about on the way upstairs?"

"Nothing, sir." The other forensics unit guys came in and reported the same, except for minute scratches inside the door lock.

"Alright then. Check with the M.E. to see if he needs anything before you head back to the station." They left without another word. "Okay, now. What's next?" he sat drinking his coffee for a second, until a man walked over to the table with a file. "Oh, yeah. Thank you, Detective. This is what we found last night from what you asked for."

"You got something from the tapes?" Adrianna asked impatiently.

"Only a vehicle. It's an extended cab truck, black, with dead tags. We couldn't get a clear picture of the license plate at all. We ran the names you gave us, but they were all dead ends. None matched the suspects. The truck was seen on the cameras at every Stop and Shop that the victims frequented. The windows are tented, but he had his window rolled down in one shot. We got one still of who we believe may be the partner." He passed the photo to Adrianna.

"I know you can't tell much from the photo, but it's all we have. And it's only a couple inches of a face. We did get access to a facial recognition software, but I had to pull a few strings. They're running it now." He took a drink of his coffee.

"Well, it's at least something. I can't see anything familiar or recognize the face, but I'm not positive I ever saw the Partner. Did you have any luck with the list Sam sent?" Adrianna asked, returning to her coffee as well.

Putting his cup down and wiping his mouth, "Yes we did. But I don't know if I'd call it luck."

"What do you mean?"

"He means, we found more than we thought we would." Sam explained.

"Bring them in!" the Chief ordered. "I had some of my guys bring them from the station. Our conference rooms aren't large anyway, so Sam said we could use this room for now." He said quietly.

A moment later, a voice rang through the hall to make room. Five detectives walked in the room carrying two or three boxes a piece, each marked Stalker Case. "When I was informed of what you were looking for, I knew you were on to something. But this, we never expected this. We expanded your search to the surrounding states, but then we saw the need to expand it nationally."

"Oh my god." She whispered.

"Yes, ma'am." Said a man, now leaning against the doorway.

"Who are you?" she asked. His slick, dark suit and errant demeanor made him appear out of place.

"Adrianna, this is Agent Carter, from the FBI. When we expanded our search nationally, and it became a federal case, the FBI gained jurisdiction."

"Really?" she said, not really asking. "So, you're just going to come in and take over the case?"

"No, ma'am. Usually, that would be the case. But seeing as how our profilers knocked down your search and it still included all of this, we're going to need as much help as we can get. These two men have wreaked havoc in every state in our country. Thanks to you, the Stalker is stopped, but we need to take the partner down as soon as we can."

Sitting silently for a moment while she drank her coffee, everyone watched her intently. Iris came through the door to the kitchen, curiosity etched on her face. She looked around at all the boxes and files.

"What's going on? The whole house got quiet all of a sudden."

"Iris, I think we're going to be occupying your dining room for longer than we thought." The Chief answered.

"How bad is it?" she asked.

Adrianna turned to the Agent. He took a paper from the top of one of the boxes and read, "From what we've found, they've been at it together for eight years. Including our newest victim, sixty-eight dead; twelve of which are from New York. We can trace the Stalkers DNA to all sixty-eight women that fell victim to his crimes. Along with the Stalker's DNA, we also found an unidentified DNA sample from thirty-three of those sixty-eight women. We're still verifying numbers of the family members taken." He paused for a moment, checking to make sure Iris didn't want to leave the room.

"Both DNA samples were also found in seventeen rape victims prior to any of the homicides. During the months of the sexual assaults, there was also multiple break-ins and robberies in the same cities. The first ones seemed to be more careless, other than the fact of the suspects wearing gloves. As the months wore on however, they honed their skill, using a lock pick or stolen spare keys for entry. We can't find anything before that, so we're assuming they met right around the time the first break-ins occurred eight years ago."

They all sat in shock, as they stared at the boxes on the table in front of them. Even Sam was visibly surprised by what the Agent said. Sixty-nine. Sixty-nine dead women, and their families, just ripped from the world. Plus, the rapes and everyone else hurt or damaged from them.

"How are you going to stop a monster like that?" Iris asked, breaking the silence.

Adrianna stood, anger boiling inside her. "The same way I stopped the Stalker."

Book 2
Written by N L Hiser

<u>Twenty-Three</u>

Alright, hold on, Adrianna." Agent Carter said, posturing. "Now, you're not going to go out here being some vigilante. This is still an FBI and police case. You're a civilian. Now, you may have stopped the Stalker, but you did it by breaking the law and killing him."

"No!" Sam stood, interrupting the FBI agent. "She chased him down after he killed one of our own. If it weren't for her, he'd still be out there with his damn partner. They could've disappeared and gotten away with it. With all of this!" he said waving his hand at the boxes and files around him. "*She* is the only reason we've come this close to ending this. And *she* is the only surviving victim."

He turned to her. "I know you don't like being called a victim, Adrianna. I can see you nearly twitch in disdain every time. I'm just trying to make a point."

"She is the only one who knows these guys personally. She can tell us things about them that none of us can guess. Even if she doesn't know it yet." He continued.

The agent twisted his lips, considering what he said. "Alright. You're right. She-I'm sorry, I mean *you* may be able to give us more information about them. Maybe something that will help us catch him. But we are not going to go after him with the intention of killing him. That's not how we do things." He sat down on the other side of the table, scooting a couple boxes over from in front of him. "We'll find him and catch him. Then he'll be locked up in prison until his trial. And with these charges, he won't be getting out."

"It may not be how you do things, but maybe that's what need to start happening. He'll escape, Carter. Just like the Stalker did. I think they had it planned for a while in case one of them gets caught."

"What makes you say that?"

"Because he told me he'd escape."

"When?" he asked, surprised.

"When the warehouse was raided. Some sort of alarm went off in the building and he came down the stairs to where the red-haired woman and I were. He broke her neck and then came over to me. He said that the cops were there, but they weren't going to save me. He said he was giving me one year to live my life or try to hide, and then he was going to escape and come find me."

He said he had been watching me for a long time and knew everything about me, so there was nowhere I could go or anything I could do, that he didn't already know I'd think about. He said he'd get me back and then he'd do what he wanted with me. That I wasn't going to die unless it was by his hands and not until he wanted me too."

The Stalker said that there was nothing I could do about it because we were destined to be together until he decided to kill me." She took a drink of her coffee. "I thought it was in my file now. I didn't tell anyone initially, but after I did, I thought it'd be put in."

"It is. Alex and I both put it in there when you told us. At the time, we didn't believe you. You were so certain he'd get out and come back for you. Understandably so. Now, I'm sorry we didn't believe you." Sam interjected.

"It's alright, Sam. I probably did just sound paranoid. Hell! I have been paranoid ever since that night. The only difference now is, I'm not afraid anymore. I know what's coming, and I know what I have to do when it's time. I won't live in fear anymore. I have for long enough."

Sam smiled a little proudly. Iris stood grinned and then suddenly turned to walk back in the kitchen. She was back with platters full of food before anyone could say another word. "Sorry, I forgot that I was about to bring these in here. Everyone eat up. You're going to need it." She said apologetically.

Everyone muttered a thank you as she then brought in plates and silverware. She soon returned to the kitchen, saying something about brewing another pot of coffee. Everyone took a few pieces as they continued on with their work, leaving Adrianna, Sam, the Chief, and Agent Carter alone in the dining room.

"Adrianna, how much of the warehouse do you remember?" the Chief asked around a bite of bacon.

"Not a lot. I kept passing out. It's all sort of a fog, like a drunken night. I can see some parts of it but it's like my brain wasn't working right when it was happening. The only times I remember being awake was while he was hurting me, and when I saw the red-haired woman right before it was raided."

"Any details about the warehouse itself or where things were? Do you remember seeing or even hearing anyone else there besides the Stalker and the woman?" Carter urged.

"No. I can't remember seeing her before, except for right before the alarm went off. And my eyes were so swollen I could barely see her at all. The warehouse…I remember a metal staircase going up to some little office looking area, trash and garbage on the floor, the smell of blood, dust, and…"

"And what?" Carter asked.

"Cigarettes. I remember the smell of cigarettes burning. And-." She grabbed her mouth, gagging.

"What's wrong?" Sam asked panicked.

She tried to take a deep breath to keep from throwing up. It didn't work. She ran to the nearest trash can and retched. The Chief offered her a napkin and she wiped the spittle from her mouth. "Are you okay, Adrianna?" Sam asked behind her.

She nodded, and after a few seconds, she continued. "Burning flesh." Her voice shook. "That's the only thing I can think would smell like that." Remembering, she cried. "He liked to use a taser and zap the bottoms of my feet. I was smelling my own rotting skin!" she exclaimed, crying.

Sam put an arm around her, trying to console her. "I'm sorry. I didn't mean to start crying. I didn't remember that before, and now I can remember the smell, perfectly."

"It's alright." The Chief said. "To have gone through what you have, well, you're stronger than I am. You don't need to apologize for crying. I would too." He grinned, reassuringly.

"Adrianna, I need to ask you something." Carter mentioned hesitantly.

"What is it?" she wiped the tears from her eyes, nodding a thank you to Sam who handed her another napkin.

"Would you be okay with going back to the warehouse?"

"Now, come on!" Sam exclaimed. "She doesn't need to go back to that place. She's already been through enough. Isn't asking her to remember stuff enough already?"

"I'm sorry, Jones. Adrianna, I don't want to put you through anything you can't handle." He said. "But like we said, you can tell us things that we can't find out any other way. I wouldn't ask unless I really needed to. And you could say no. Honestly, I wouldn't blame you if you did. But it could jog a memory that you didn't know you had."

"The M.E.'s report did say that the Stalkers lungs looked clean, like he had never smoked. So maybe the partner did. If you could smell the cigarettes, maybe you seen him and didn't know it." The Chief added.

"But my eyes were almost swollen shut. Even if I had seen him, I doubt I could tell you anything about what he looked like."

"You'd be surprised. I'll bring one of my profilers with us, and a sketch artist. She'll be able to help guide you through your memories, and just might be able to find something that can help. If you're willing to. It's completely up to you." Carter said, sitting back in his chair.

"Excuse me, sir?" a young man in a cop uniform walked through the doorway.

"Yes?" the Chief answered.

"A neighbor found this on their car when they came outside. It's addressed to Miss Davidson." He handed it over.

Adrianna took it from the Chief. "It's from the partner. He likes to call me by my old name to taunt me."

"Wait, Adrianna." Carter took a pair of gloves from the box on the corner of the table. "If you really want to read it, fine. But put these on so we can check it for prints when you're done."

Nodding, she quickly pulled on the gloves and gently removed the envelope from the evidence bag. It was completely soaked through from the rain, with a line of dirt across the front presumably from the car. "It's too wet." She said. "It's going to tear."

Iris turned around from placing a cup of coffee on the table for the Agent. "Hold on. Give me just a second." She ran upstairs as fast as she could and returned shortly after with a blow-dryer. "Here."

"Thank you!"

Sam plugged it in beside the buffet table and turned it on. Being careful not to tear it, they laid it on the evidence bag and swept the dryer over it. After a few minutes, it was dry enough.

Adrianna picked it up and very gently, opened the envelope. Slowly, she pulled out a small, folded paper. The Agent hurriedly pulled on gloves and took the envelope, placing it back in the evidence bag. She carefully unfolded the paper, with the men reading over her shoulder.

The ink was slightly faded and smeared from the rain, but she seen it was still legible. She read, "Hello, *Katherine*. I wonder…did you like the gift I left you? I made sure it was somewhere you'd find it… She was a fighter… Not unlike you… You can see it written all over her pretty face now… That's not the only thing you have in common, is it?… No…my friend didn't tell you, did he?… So sad…You should have known…He didn't love you, you know…your husband…no. We found them together you see…when he should've been home…taking care of you…being a man."

Instead, he was with her…She's not the only one... The red head woman was another of his... So, I guess…this really is a gift for you…the dead, mutilated body of one of your husband's whores. Plus, you got to see the other die... personally. If you don't believe me…I guess… you'll just have to see for yourself…soon enough. I've enjoyed this little game…*Katherine*. But I want to play a new game now…Can you guess what I'm thinking?… See you soon…*Katherine*."

She handed the letter to Carter and sank down into her chair. No one said a word, instead they only waited for her to say something. After five minutes had past, Sam spoke up.

"Adrianna?"

"Yeah?"

"Um…are you alright?" he glanced around to the other men, not knowing what to expect.

"Yeah."

"Are you sure?"

"What?" she looked up at him. "Yes, I'm fine. I'm just trying to think what he's thinking."

"Huh?" the Chief said, surprised.

"He asked me to guess what he's thinking. So, I'm trying to think about it."

"But-."

"Yeah, I know. I read it. We were having troubles for a year before this all happened. I suspected he was talking to someone else, but I didn't think he was the type to cheat. I guess I was wrong. Either way, worrying about that won't help us now." She sat straight. "Carter, let's go to the warehouse."

"Are you sure?" he asked, his brows raised.

"Yes. Let's do it."

"Okay." Looking at the Chief, "Have your people go through these files. We need to find out how the suspects targeted these specific victims. If we can figure that out, we might know where to look for the partner." His phone rang, and he excused himself from the room.

Adrianna ran upstairs to change and grab a coat. She bent down to the carrier and took Tiger out. Giving him a kiss and some much-needed attention, she then returned him to the carrier and left the room. Finding Iris in the living room, sitting on the couch with her feet up finally resting, she went and sat down beside her.

"Iris, do you mind letting Tiger out of his carrier later, as soon the others leave, and the doors are closed? I don't want him stuck in the carrier all day."

"Of course, honey. Sam just told me you're about to go back to the warehouse. Are you sure you want to do that?"

"Yeah. I need to. Not just for the case, but for me. I need to know. We have to stop him."

"Okay. If you need me, just call me, alright? You have my number?"

"Yes." She smiled. She gave her a hug goodbye and walked back to the dining room to find Agent Carter.

Finding Sam and the Chief still there, she asked, "Hey, did Agent Carter come back in?"

As if on cue, he walked through the kitchen doorway into the room. "We have a name."

"What?" she asked, incredulous.

"Facial recognition just came back. The partner's name is Edward 'Eddie' Miller. His background information is being faxed here now. We still don't have a name on the Stalker, but they're running his face through the system now."

"Any address?"

"No. But now that we have his name, we're looking for his work history, past addresses, et cetera."

"Good. Let's go."

"Wait!" said Sam. "Don't you want to know his background?"

"Yes, but you can call and tell us when we're on the road. We still need to find out how they met. If we can do that, we can get the Stalker's name and background if the facial recognition search doesn't work. We can't sit around and just hope it works. We need to try the warehouse." She said, already heading for the door.

"Okay but be careful." Sam yelled after her.

Twenty-Four

Eddie Miller watched Adrianna get **in** the SUV with the suits as he sat on a porch down the street. The owners wouldn't be home from work for hours, so he didn't worry. Besides, no one knew who he was or what he looked like. To them, he was a ghost. Something Wright had taught him well.

He grinned as he watched them drive away. "Where are you heading to, Katherine? Going out looking for me? Ha-ha! Good luck! You won't find me until I want you to. Oh, but I'll be watching you. Ha-ha! Yes. I'll be watching you and all your pig friends."

He sat and smiled as the rain began to lighten. He rocked back in the antique rocking chair obviously handed down through the family residing in the house, and the creaks filled the air with the rain. Thunder rumbled in the distance as he lit another cigarette and pulled. He swigged the rest of his beer and exhaled the camel's smoke. He smiled again, showing his stained and rotting teeth.

"Umm... maybe it's time I have a little fun." He grinned. He twisted off the metal cap of another bottle of Natural Ice and took a large swig. "Oh yeah. It's time to a have a little fun."

Twenty-Five

The rain was nothing more than a drizzle now, running over the windows of the SUV as they drove away. She could see it recede in the leaf filled, flooded ditches along the streets they passed. As they drove past a tree with leaves the color of copper and crimson, she was reminded of Sara. She would have to remember to call her later. Surely, she'd be mad if she didn't let her know what was happening.

They weaved through the streets toward the warehouse they had found her at, over a year ago. It was odd how over a year ago, she spent who knows how many hours there, and she couldn't remember most of it. She remembered none of the time she spent being wheeled out on the gurney and into an ambulance, and then transported to the hospital. But that makes sense, she remembered. Sam said I died twice on the way to the hospital. Of course, I wouldn't remember that.

She stared out of the window, not really paying attention to what was outside. Instead, she wondered why she hadn't seen her daughter when she died. Maybe there really isn't a heaven or a hell, she mused. If there was, surely my daughter would have been let in the gates. And me, I would've thought I'd make it there. At least to say goodbye to her one last time.

Her phone rang, startling her from her thoughts. She answered it and put it on speaker after realizing it was Sam. "Hey, Sam." She said.

"Hey. Okay, the fax is in. Ready for this?"

"Go ahead." Said Agent Carter.

"So, Edward Miller was the oldest child of a prostitute who overdosed when he was twelve. She died in their trailer in Kansas, and he and his younger siblings were then placed in the care of his uncle. After multiple run-ins with the law for stealing, and calls to the home for domestic abuse, and physical abuse of the kids, the police and CPS workers arrived at the home to remove the children, only to find out that he and his oldest sister had ran away."

They found her a week later when she turned herself into the cops saying her brother tried to hold her down and touch her, so she hit him and ran away. He wasn't seen or heard of again until he was twenty. He got hired for a job at a gas station in Waco, Texas but on his second day, was asked to take a routine drug test the following morning. The manager reported that he said he'd be there, but never showed. He went off the grid after that." Sam told them.

"Damn." Adrianna said.

"Yeah. I'm sending the only picture of him on file to your phone now. It was taken when he was…let me see here, thirteen. So, when he lived with his uncle. Also, something that popped up when his background came through. His uncle that they lived with, was arrested and charged a month later for sexual assault of a minor on his younger sibling, his brother, who was ten at the time."

"No wonder he's so fucked up." She muttered.

"Yeah." Sam said, through the phone. "Let me know if you need anything. And Iris said she'll have lunch ready for you when you get back."

She smiled, chuckling. "Will do. Thanks. See you soon."

"Bye."

"Goodbye." They replied, and she hung up the call.

The drive took them another twenty minutes, reaching the outskirts of Staten Island. A minute later, they pulled up to a warehouse, right by the water.

"Here we are."

"Hmm."

"What is it?"

"I didn't remember the water."

"I would be surprised if you did. But the only warehouses on Staten Island are on the outskirts, by the water. Only one is still up and running now. The rest are either torn down or will be soon, like this one. Are you ready to go inside?"

Looking up through the drizzle at the building as it loomed over them, she felt a pang in her gut. Taking a deep breath, she nodded and followed him in. As they entered the front door, they were hit by a pungent odor of dried blood and rat feces. The air seemed stale, as if the building hadn't been opened in a long time. The floor was covered in trash and other filth she was certain she didn't want to touch.

"Wow. Be careful not to touch anything. It could be evidence, but honestly, from the looks of this place, I'm more worried about needing a tetanus shot." He told her. He scooted something on the floor out of his way, only to step away from it quickly, as if something had crawled out of it. "At the very least, a good shower. Eh!"

She almost laughed, until a rat ran past her foot screeching. She sidestepped as fast as she could, almost knocking over Carter. "Sorry."

"You're good. We won't be here long." He said. "Can you show me where you were?" he asked.

Looking around for a few minutes and walking down a small hall that opened into a room, she exclaimed, "Over here!" She spotted the office looking area and headed toward it carefully.

Carter followed close behind her. Once they got closer and traversed the piles of garbage that were undeniably dwelling remains of vagrants, they stood in front of the stairs. She turned around, scanning the area in front of her.

"I was there." She said as she slowly walked over to the table. "I didn't expect the table to still be here. I thought it'd be in evidence."

"The report said it was welded to the floor. Without the equipment on hand, I doubt the police department could take it into evidence."

"Oh." She replied, staring at the table. Just then, the door opened, and two agents walked in. Carter called them over. Looking at them standing around her, she turned back to the table. "What do you want to know?"

The profiler spoke behind her. "Close your eyes and take a deep breath." Hearing Adrianna exhale slowly she continued. "Now, it's night. You just heard your daughter scream-."

"Wait. I thought you wanted me to remember what happened *here*."

"Shh... relax. Trust me. We need to start at your last memory before this place."

"Okay." She scratched her leg with her foot.

"Take a deep breath. Relax. Now, go back to that night. She just screamed, and you and your husband came running in. Your daughter's on the floor. Your husband wrestles with him and then falls to the floor. What do you do?"

"I screamed and ran over to him. I was sitting between their bodies, crying, screaming."

"Then what happened?" she asked.

"He hit me in the head. The pain was horrible. Then, everything just went black. I passed out."

"He carried you down the stairs, out the door, and into a vehicle. Can you see what kind it is?"

"No, I was knocked out."

"Sometimes when we pass out, we can still hear things around us. Sometimes even see things happening in little slivers of time. It's our body's way of trying to protect us. To get into flight or fight mode. Just try and see."

She took another deep breath. "I could hear talking. At first, I thought it was a dream. It was really low, like whispering. I smelled a cigarette burning... A car door opening... He put me in the backseat, but he had to lift me up higher than usual to do it. And it was small. Only enough room to lay a person. Not much more."

"Okay. That sounds like he put you in a truck. Maybe a smaller one with a cab in the back."

"Yeah. It felt like the seat was wrapped in something. It was noisy when I moved and uncomfortable... I could hear the door close and then the front doors open... The doors closed... Then he turned the truck on... I can't remember anything else." She shook her head, trying to focus.

"That's alright." She said, placing a hand on Adrianna's shoulder. "What's the next thing you remember?"

She tried to go forward in her memories, tried to recognize something, anything. "My head started hurting again when we went over a bump... I think I groaned when the back tires went over it. One of them turned around to make sure I was still out... He mumbled something, but I couldn't understand him... Then, the truck stopped, but I rolled out of the seat and into the little bit of floor. I could hear him cuss and open his door, and then the back door. He pulled me out and dropped me on the ground... Gravel. It hurt."

"Good." She whispered. "Keep going."

She tried to ignore the profiler's comment. She had said it like she was glad it hurt. She shook her head and tried to focus, knowing that yelling at her wouldn't help anyone.

"I could hear him yelling at the partner. Telling him that he had to carry me now. One of them picked me up and swung me over his shoulder. I could hear the gravel crunching under their feet as they walked. With each footstep, my head swung painfully until I passed out again." She took a deep breath, focusing on going farther. "When I woke up again, I was on the table. My hands were handcuffed above my head, and my ankles were bound. I couldn't tell by what then, but I found out yesterday that it was leather straps."

"That's good. Keep going. Don't focus on what he does to you. Focus on what you hear and see around you. Can you see the partner?"

She nodded slowly. "He cut my clothes off. But then he disappeared. There were lights. Like the one's workers use outside in the dark. They circled this area here." She said, opening her eyes and pointing to where they were. "There was a cart type of thing...here."

"What was on it?"

"Everything. All the things they used on me." Shaking the image from the front of her mind, she continued. "There was a small generator by the corner there and it looked like they had swept all the garbage to behind the lights, so it wasn't on the floor around here. I can't remember anything else from around here. I remember hearing them talking up there. I saw smoke coming through that hole." She pointed up to the office and the slot hole between the glass window and the wall. "I could see a light coming from inside." She said as she started to walk up the stairs, the others followed close enough behind that the profiler's hand never left her shoulder. "I could see some sort of table inside, through the door, but I couldn't see much more."

They made it to the top stair and stepped up onto the small landing. "Wait, Adrianna." Carter said. "We don't know what's inside. Let me check it out first."

"It's been over a year. You don't really think he, or anything dangerous could be inside, do you?" she responded, only hesitating for a second. She pushed the door gently, and the door swung open, the rusted metal henge creaked loudly. Stepping inside, she moved to the wall, so the others could come in as well. "It's too dark. I can't see anything."

The sketch artist held up his phone and turned on its flashlight. "Thanks." The others muttered. They pushed forward slowly, careful to watch their step of any debris on the floor. Directly in front of the door, on the opposite wall, sat the table she remembered. Papers scattered on the floor under it, but nothing was left on it besides the old nearly bare spots where dust was swept away for whatever items used to be there but were being slowly layered with dust again. She could see a foreboding dark red splatter of what she assumed was dried blood, that covered almost half of the table. In the corner sat a folding chair with an old glass ash tray underneath it, nearly covered with the debris that filled most of the building.

"It looks like they took everything with them." Carter said.

"I figured they would." She responded. "They're too smart for that. Well, at least the Stalker was. But it looks like the partner may have missed something." She walked over to the chair and motioned Carter over. "Look." She pointed at the ash tray sitting below it.

"I wonder if they left any prints on it. It is glass, so maybe?"

"There's a good chance." He said. He reached in his coat pocket and pulled out a latex glove and evidence bag.

"Do you guys always carry gloves and bags with you?" she asked amused.

"Usually." He answered. Careful not to touch it with his hand and only his glove, he picked it up and put it in the bag. Sealing it, he continued.

"It's always better to be safe than sorry. I've been in the law enforcement industry for a little over twenty years now. I can't tell you how many times I've come across something randomly or get called to a scene in the middle of the night. It's good to keep them on hand just in case I need them."

"Sort of like a gun. Rather have it and not need it, than need it and not have it."

"Exactly." Cocking his head to the side, he retorted, "I think I've heard that in a movie somewhere."

Laughing she turned back to the room. "There's not much in here. So, what else do you want me to try to remember?"

"Well," said the profiler. "Let's go back to the table. What's the next thing you remember after he cut off your clothes?"

She nodded her head and walked back out to the table down the stairs. Once there she closed her eyes and concentrated. "He was smiling at me. I remember how disgusted I was, because he was drooling a little when he cut them off. It dripped onto my stomach. He just smirked when he seen me jerk away. I could see nasty teeth and feel his hot garbage breath."

Then the Stalker walked down the stairs and he backed away from me. He told him to 'go get it'. I wasn't sure what he meant until he came back with a syringe. I was still groggy, but I was trying not to let myself pass out again. The Stalker took it from him and stuck me in my neck. I can remember the pain. It burned like he shot a needle full of lava inside me."

Everything started becoming a little clearer though. My heart raced. I started to grow afraid of what he gave me. Then he leaned over really close, I could feel his hot breath on my cheek. He smelled like Axe body spray and licorice. He said, 'it's just a little something to keep you awake for a while. You're not going to want to sleep through what happens next.' I tried to yell at him, but that's when I realized they had gagged me with some sort of strap of fabric. He laughed and went to take it out of my mouth, but I head butted him. He got pissed and punched me. I passed out again."

"What was the partner doing during this?"

"He sat on the bottom of the stairs, just watching and smoking a cigarette."

"Can you tell us what he looked like?" Carter interjected.

She nodded slowly and closed her eyes. The sketch artist quickly took out his pad and pencil. "Five, nine or ten. About the same height as the Stalker. His hair was dark, maybe black. Long enough that he had it slicked back with gel or something. Five o'clock shadow. Really pale. Sunken eyes. They were…really dark brown. I remember from him leaning over me. He was bulky. Not fat, but he was solid. He looked like he grew up learning to fight in the streets. Square jaw. He sweat a lot. I could smell it on him constantly. He was always wiping himself with a bandana. He had a real sleaze ball feel to him."

The sketch artist drew for a few minutes and then showed her. "What do you think?"

"That's him."

"Good. Now what do you think about us getting out of here?" Carter asked, smiling.

"Yeah, let's go." She said, taking one last glance around the building. They turned to leave and started making their way towards the door again. She glanced at the stairs as she passed them. "Wait!"

"What? What's wrong?" he asked spinning around, hand on his holster.

"The partner has a tattoo!"

"What? How do you know?"

"I saw it. Sometime after that, the Stalker had done something to me and then turned to walk to the stairs. The partner was there sitting and watching, so he got up and started walking up in front of the Stalker. I remember raising my head up, looking around but only seeing bits and pieces because I had blood in one of my eyes. But I saw it! He has a spider tattooed on the back of his neck!"

"That's awesome news. We can use that to help identify him when we catch him, and he stands trial. Good work, Adrianna. You've gave us a lot of information here." He smiled. "Come on. Let's get out of here."

She nodded, taking Carter's arm as she quickly stepped over a pile of garbage that seemed to be moving. "Yeah, let's get out of here before we get bit by a rat." She joked.

Book 2
Written by N L Hiser

Twenty-Six

By the time they made it back to **the** house, most of the uniforms had left to go back to the station. The sketch artist that had met them at the warehouse, drew up a sketch of the spider tattoo and then left for the station as well, while the profiler joined them inside. She stayed right with her and Adrianna couldn't help but feel that the woman was there to profile her, as much as to profile the killers. Trying not to be rude, in case she was wrong, she ignored her tag-along and tried to act as if she didn't notice nor care.

Iris met her in the kitchen where she grabbed a bottle of water. "Hey. What are you up to?" she asked her.

"My friend arrived a few minutes ago. Do you want to go do that after you eat?" Iris asked, eyeing the profiler.

"Great. Yeah, that sounds good. Where is she?"

"She went to the bathroom, but you can probably find her in the living room with her bag in a minute."

"Cool." Noticing how Iris kept glancing behind her, she added. "This is the profiler Carter mentioned. Though, I don't think I caught her name." she said, turning to the woman.

"Oh, I'm Agent Garcia. I'm sorry." The woman laughed. "I didn't realize Carter didn't tell you. We kind of just got right to work."

"True." Adrianna nodded. "Help yourself to something to drink, Agent Garcia. I need to go help someone real fast. Otherwise, it'd be rude." And without another word, she quickly left the room.

She walked into the living room, finding a woman around her forties, sitting on the couch scrolling through something on her phone. She was a pretty woman all done up like you'd expect from any well-respecting cosmetologist. Remembering that Iris never gave her the woman's name, she hesitated for a second, to think of what to say. Deciding, she approached the woman.

"Hi! You must be Iris' friend."

She looked up from her phone, smiling with a genuine kindness in her eyes, and stood. "Hi! Yes, I'm Susan. She told me you're looking to change up your look?"

"Yes, ma'am. I need your help. But I need to ask you not to tell anyone what you do here, or anything you hear while you're here. It's important that no one finds out yet."

"Well, I can do that for sure. But why does it need to be so hush-hush?"

"Have you seen the news?"

"Of course, but I don't believe everything I hear on there. The news is always lying about stuff, so unless I've seen it myself, I'm not going to believe it."

"Oh, well, good. I'm Katherine Davidson, though I go by Adrianna Swift now."

"Oh. So, all those FBI people and cops were here for you?"

"Sort of. Iris' husband, Sam is a detective on the case. One of the ones that rescued me. I'm back in town now trying to help them close the case. But I need a new look so that the press won't recognize me. Plus, I sort of need it for myself too."

"I completely understand, girl. Don't worry about it. Nobody will hear a thing from me."

"I appreciate it."

"So, do you know what you're looking for?"

Adrianna gave her a crooked smile. "I do. Did you bring your stuff?"

"Of course. I even brought dye, just in case."

"Excellent. Well, I just got back and we're all about to eat lunch. So, would you like to come eat with us? We can then do it after."

"Sounds good to me. What's Iris making?"

"Honestly, I don't know. But she's a hell of a cook."

"Oh, I know girl." She laughed. "Let's go find her."

"Cool. Come on."

They walked back through the dining room and into the kitchen looking for Iris. As they came in, they were hit by a wave of mouthwatering aroma. Iris was bent over, pulling three large pans of cheese steak sandwiches from the oven. Hurrying, Adrianna grabbed a couple of extra dishtowels from a drawer and helped her pull them out and place them on the table she had already covered.

"Mm, these smell and look amazing, Iris." Susan said, closing the oven for them.

"Oh, it's nothing. They're pretty quick and easy to make. I just like putting them together and them placing them in the oven for a minute or two for the cheese to melt and bread to toast a bit." Just then the deep fryer's alarm went off, beeping loudly. "Oh!" she exclaimed. Pulling out the double baskets, she said, "The fries are ready too."

"You do too much, Iris." Adrianna said. "At least let me order dinner for everyone tonight. This is the second big meal you've cooked today, and you haven't had much of a break, running around making sure everyone has had drinks and things."

"Oh, please. It's fine."

"I know. And I'm positive everyone appreciates it. You're an amazing cook, and hostess. But you need a break every once in a while, too. You're at least going to sit with us and eat, right?"

"Well, I need to do the dishes and-."

"Nope. You're eating with us." Susan interrupted.

Adrianna could see the defeat in Iris's eyes. "Alright. I'll take a break."

"Thank you." They both responded.

They arranged plates, silverware, cups, and anything else needed around the kitchen, then they walked into the dining room. Adrianna asked everyone to clear everything off the table for lunch, and to her surprise, they easily agreed. Everyone got it cleared quickly, and then went to the kitchen to make themselves a plate.

They sat around the table eating and chatting, being careful not to talk about the case. It seemed everyone needed a small break from contemplating their next moves. She sat for a while, eating in silence but legitimately enjoying listening to the conversations around her. Sam and his buddies from work were talking about a football game coming up and who they thought stood the best chance at winning. Agent Carter and his team talked about what their plans were for the coming holidays, all looking forward to their allotted time off work for the first time in a long time. Susan and Iris exchanged gossip, Susan giving away things her clients at Sissy's salon had divulged.

Suddenly, she realized she was being watched by Agent Garcia's eagle like gaze. She turned her gaze right back, pensive. She knew that Carter had probably told her to keep a close eye on her, but she wasn't going to be intimidated. Instead of her turning away however, she smiled and continued to watch her. A bit perplexed, she decided to ignore her. She turned her attention to Iris and Susan, asking them how long they've known each other. They giggled, saying they met each other years ago. They went on to tell her about how their brothers used to play football together.

"So, Adrianna, what are you planning to do for the holidays?" the profiler asked, interrupting the conversation. The room grew silent, and Adrianna could see everyone exchanging glances.

"Um, I don't know yet." She said shaking her head slowly. "Thanksgiving is just a few weeks away, but I don't know how long it'll take to get this case closed. I know I'm going back to my place in Luray after this."

"You won't be spending them with your family, then?"

Carter interrupted. "Agent Garcia, I don't think you should-."

"No…have you read my file, yet? Because if you had, you'd know I have no living family members left, and my husband's family never really liked me anyhow. So, no. I will not be spending the holidays with family. Will *you*, Agent Garcia?" She pushed back, biting out every word.

"Yes, I am. But that's not what this is about. I was curious as to what you'll be doing with your time since you won't have family around. I never meant to be obtrusive. I was only curious."

Adrianna paused, trying to keep from flipping out on the woman. She forced herself to take a long, steadying breath. "Look, when this is all done, I'm going back home. Until then, I'm here. And I'll be working on this case with all of you. But anything I do, or plan to do outside of this case, is none of your business. Regardless whether you've been instructed to 'keep an eye on me' or not. You're not here to profile me. So, do your real job and stay out of my head."

Everyone froze and glanced between the two of them, not knowing what to expect next. Agent Garcia glanced quickly to Carter, and then back to Adrianna. "I wasn't profiling you, Adrianna. I was just-."

"For a profiler, you're a shitty liar. Just stay out of my head, stop following me around, and help us find the partner. Do that, and we'll be fine."

She lowered her eyes, knowing she was stuck. "Alright."

"Good." Adrianna said, forcibly ending the conversation. She took another bite of her food. Everyone sat quietly, finishing their food. After a moment, she couldn't help it anymore. "These are great, Iris." She said. Everyone muttered a 'yeah it's great' and a 'thank you', following her lead. Iris blushed and thanked everyone.

Soon, everyone was back to their conversations and enjoying their meal. Adrianna could finally breathe a sigh of relief as she could feel the tension leave the room. A few short minutes later, she walked to the kitchen to put her dishes away. As soon as Susan was finished, she motioned for her to follow her upstairs to her room.

Twenty-Seven

Eddie Miller laid back on the old mattress he had found in the old, abandoned house. It was filthy and smelled of urine, but he was thankful to have a comfortable bed for the night ahead. He had had worse. He was used to living in dirty slums, and though he had seen a few tiny bugs crawling on it before he laid down, he was only glad the cops hadn't been called after he broke in the window. He really didn't feel like dealing with police. I'd have to take out the pigs, he mused. I have too much to do still. I don't want them ruining it.

He laid staring at the ceiling above him, picturing his hands around Katherine's throat. I'm going to choke her to death. He smiled. Soon anyways. I can't wait to get rid of that bitch. She ruined everything. Now, I'm going to have to kill her and leave state for good this time. Start fresh somewhere else. His glanced toward the end of the mattress, to the half-naked body of the prostitute he had brought with him. At least she made the wait a little better, he chuckled to himself.

His eyes slid closed as he imagined where he'd head to next, and all the fun he'd have there. He smiled and dreamed of his next exploits happily.

<u>Twenty-Eight</u>

Iris and Adrianna helped Susan load **her** things into her car and hugged her goodbye. She made sure to tip her well and thanked her for helping her. Susan slid into the driver's seat as Adrianna closed the door behind her, and the two waved her off as she pulled away down the street.

"Thanks for calling her, Iris. I appreciate it. She seems like a good woman."

"She is. And an even better friend. I like your hair. It fits you."

"Really? I've never gone so short before, so I was a little nervous. But I think I like it."

"I love it. I think it looks great on you. What's the style called?"

"I don't know what it's actually called. I just showed her a picture I found online. It's just a short-cropped style with extra length on the top. What do you think of the color?"

"I love it. It has just enough of the red hue in it now, that you can't be certain of the original color."

"Good. I decided to get it cut like this because I figured with it being so short, it could make my face shape appear a little different. That way, I can *maybe* disguise my round face and brown hair a little."

"Well, it works. And you look younger. I loved your hair before, but somehow, it made you look almost ten years older than you are. This looks more your age. It makes me want to cut my hair now too." She laughed.

"Thanks. So, do you think it'll fool the press?"

"Absolutely! I doubt anyone would recognize you now. Especially if they've only seen a photo of you before all this happened."

"Perfect." She smiled, happy. The wind picked up and hit them with another cold gust. "It sure feels colder now without all my hair." She laughed.

"Let's get inside." Iris smiled and hooked her arm in Adrianna's as they headed back in.

They walked quietly into the dining room and waited in the doorway as they watched everyone work. A couple of seconds later, Sam looked up and caught his wife's gaze and smiled back.

"Hi, honey. Was that Susan I heard leaving?"

"Yeah, she's headed home."

He glanced at Adrianna and paused, his eyes widening. "Adrianna, you look…"

"Amazing!" Garcia's voice piping up unexpectedly drew her attention. The agent immediately lowered her eyes, cheeks flushed.

"Thanks." Adrianna muttered. Suddenly, she realized why the woman had been so curious, and she felt the heat rise in her face too. A small smile curved her lips as she brushed her fingers through her newly cut hair awkwardly.

Turning her attention back to Sam, she cleared her throat and added, "I thought it was time for a change. And hopefully one that will make me a little less recognizable to the press."

"It's perfect." Sam smiled. "I doubt anyone will recognize you."

"That's for sure." The Chief added.

"You look great, Adrianna. But...this may cause an issue with finding the partner."

"How?" Iris asked.

"He means it could piss him off." Adrianna answered for him. "Since they both have liked to follow me. Right?" Carter nodded. "I already thought of that, and truth be told, I don't care. I needed this change as much for being in incognito as needing something different for myself. Plus, worst case scenario, it pisses him off and he makes a mistake. And that could be exactly what we need right now to find him." She pulled out her phone and quickly took a selfie in her new do, sending it to Sara. "Now, if you all will excuse me, I need to call

Sara." And with that, she quickly smiled at Sam and Iris, and then disappeared around the corner.

"Who's Sara?" Carter asked.

"Oh, Sara's a friend of hers. They met when she was jumping state to state before heading home to Luray. They seem to have gotten pretty close."

"Yeah, I'm glad she found someone out there when she needed someone the most. And now, she'll need her again, when all this is over. I have a feeling she hasn't had time to grieve or even let herself go through the motions. They'll all hit her when it's over. It'll be nice knowing that when she leaves and heads home, she'll have a close friend with her." Iris added.

"What do you mean?" the Chief raised his brows.

"She said that they've been planning on hanging out since she settled in at Luray but hadn't found the right time yet. So, when it's all done, Sara's going to go stay with her for a while.

"Oh. That's good." The Chief said, returning to the pile of papers in front of him. His phone vibrated on the table. Reading a text, he cleared his throat. "I need to head home for a bit. Get a shower, check in with my wife, see the kids. I'll be back in a few hours."

"Tell Judy we said hello." Iris smiled.

"Will do." He grinned and left.

Twenty-Nine

Hey!"

"Hey! Oh my god! I just got your text. You look amazing! I can't believe you cut all of your hair off. Did you cry? I know girls who do when they get their hair cut a lot shorter." Sara blurted as soon as she picked up.

"No." Adrianna laughed. "It's just hair. It'll grow back. I might even grow it back out next year; I don't know."

"You said you were going to get your hair cut and change it up a bit, but this is more than a bit. I love it. You look hot with short hair!" she exclaimed.

The Adrianna Swift Series
Swift Snake

"Oh, so I didn't with my long hair?" she teased.

"I loved your long hair. I think you're beautiful. You know that. I'll always love you, no matter what you do. But this new style? And the red? You look confident and badass. And that's just sexy."

"Oh, well thank you." She giggled as she reclined back on the couch. "So, what have you been in to?"

"Oh, you know me. Just the usual."

"You still seeing that guy?"

"Oh, no. We're done."

"What happened?"

"He thought he could have me and run around at the bar in town with whoever he wanted. So, I ended it. I'm not one to deal with that crap."

"I don't blame you a bit."

"Yeah. Well, tell me what you're up to. I'm sure it's a lot more exciting over there."

"Well, we had a bit of an eventful couple days. I told you about the letter with the ring in it, and how it belongs to a missing woman we assumed the partner has, right?"

"Right."

"Well…he surprised us in the middle of the night. He broke into the house and then put her body on the front doorstep."

"Oh my god! Are you okay?"

"Yeah, I'm fine. He broke in, but we can't find anything that he's messed with. He did leave another letter though. This time it was on a neighbor's car."

"What did it say? Did you even read it?"

"Yeah. I wanted to know what he had to say. Besides, he seems different than the Stalker. Not as smart, but different. But he did tell me one thing in the letter. I was right about my husband. Well, late husband. He was cheating on me. Supposedly, the partner chose her because she was *one* of my husband's mistresses."

"Holy shit! Wait. *One* of his mistresses?"

"Yep. Apparently, her and the red headed woman from the warehouse I was rescued from."

"Oh wow. I'm sorry, Hun. I guess she sort of deserved it then, right?"

"No. No one deserves to be tortured. And this woman's family didn't deserve to be killed for her stupidity." She remembered the look on the woman's face and shivered.

"Are you alright?"

"Yeah. What's done is done."

"So... what happens now?"

"Well, for starters, we have the partner's name. Edward Miller. Goes by Eddie. Fucked up past. Sam and I were working on a few leads; we ended up finding more that we bargained for. These guys have been doing this for a long time, all over the country. And that makes it a federal case now, so the FBI are here now too."

"Are they trying to push you out of the case?"

"No…actually, we've all been working on it together since this morning. Iris has been running around cooking and cleaning, being the best hostess in the world." She laughed a little, but then remembered the partner's face. "I went back to the warehouse today."

"Really? Why?"

"To try to remember. We finally have the partners name, but he went off the grid, so we didn't have a recent photo of him. And we figured he was there in the warehouse and I just didn't remember."

"And did you?"

"Yeah, I did. More than I thought."

"Are you alright?"

"Yeah. I think so." She answered quietly, smiling, feeling lucky to have Sara in her life. "We found out some new stuff though. Things that might help us find him."

"Like what?"

"He's got a spider tattoo on the back of his neck."

"Really? Why would anyone get a tattoo of a spider? Ew!"

Adrianna chuckled. "I don't know. Maybe it was just a random thing he got a tattoo of. But, honestly, I feel like it's got to have some sort of significance for him. Neither one of them seem like they do anything randomly. Otherwise they'd have been caught sooner than this."

"Hmm, true." She could hear Sara getting more comfortable as she moved what she assumed were blankets. After a minute or so of their silent reverie, Sara added. "You know, I just thought of something. Are you positive that the newest letter was written by the partner?"

"Yeah. Why?"

"Well…if the Stalker was in prison, how did he write and send you letters? I'm sure the partner helped somehow, but didn't you say that the Stalker wasn't allowed to write or send letters while he was locked up?"

"Yeah…you're right. They must've had help on the inside or something. I don't know. I'll look into it." She smiled, scoffing. "You are really great, you know that? You always point out something I hadn't thought of."

"Why, thank you. You know, you're pretty great to, Hun. Don't sell yourself short. You're amazing. Remember what I told you."

"I know. 'I was put through these things because I'm one of the only people on earth strong enough to endure it. It doesn't make it fair, but it does make me special.' I remember."

"Good. You are special, Adrianna. You were put into this situation for a reason. And maybe that reason isn't clear yet. But there is a reason."

"Thanks, Sara." She sighed as she rubbed her back. "So, how was your day?"

"Hun, it's only four o'clock."

Adrianna looked at her phone and laughed. "Sorry, it's been a long day."

Sara giggled. "I know, I'm only picking at you. It was a normal, uneventful day here. So far. You need some sleep, girl. Maybe a massage and a shot of Jack."

Adrianna giggled. "Yeah. That'd be nice. Maybe we can get a bottle when we get back to Luray."

The Adrianna Swift Series
Swift Snake

"Definitely! Tell you what, you catch this bastard, I'll buy us a bottle when you pick me up. When we get back to your place in Luray, we'll relax and drink a little. We'll celebrate and blow off some steam. You deserve it."

"That sounds perfect. I can't wait to get out of here. I love the Jones', but I miss my little house. And I miss spending time with you. Plus, I'm so ready to put this part of my life behind me."

"I know, honey. Soon. But first, you still have work to do."

Thirty

After Adrianna said goodbye to Sara, she felt an instant ping of loneliness. She loved Sara and longed for her to be by her side. The case couldn't end fast enough. She was so done with the horrible part of her life, and she was all too ready to turn the page to the next chapter.

Adrianna looked at her phone, wishing Sara were still on the other end, before she glanced at the time and realized it was close to dinner time. Sighing tiredly, she decided to call and place an order for delivery. I need to do it now before Iris gets bored and decides to start cooking dinner, she chuckled to herself.

Hanging up the phone a few minutes later, she sighed, exhausted as she went to check on Tiger. Not finding him upstairs, she walked back down and checked the living room and dining room.

No one had seen him for a while, so she continued her search into the kitchen. As she wandered through the door, Agent Carter bumped into her.

Instantly, Adrianna gasped as she remembered her walk in Petersburg, and how it had started raining. The memory flashed in front of her eyes, as if she were reliving it. It had started thundering and she had decided to hurry back to the house. Wanting to get out of the rain and knowing Sara was coming soon, she wasn't paying attention. She was just trying to hurry and get back before it poured down on her.

A man had run into her wearing a black leather jacket. She remembered he had given her the creeps a little, but she was trying to continue to walk away. He muttered something about the storm coming soon, she had hastily apologized, and without another word, he turned around with his head ducked down and continued walking in the opposite direction. That's when she had seen it. A tattoo on the back of his neck. A spider!

She remembered the storm was raging by the time she had gotten back to the house. And she had found the letter on the doorstep when she made it up the small porch. Sara arrived a minute or two later, when she was trying to open the letter and cut herself when she heard Sara bang on the door. The partner! He had dropped off the letter just before she made it home! He was the man she had run into! He was right there! Why hadn't I realized he had a partner then when he was still locked up? She yelled at herself.

"Adrianna? Adrianna!" Carter yelled at her, breaking her train of thought.

"Huh? What? Oh, sorry. Didn't see you there." She uttered quietly, physically shaking herself out of her stupor.

"Yeah, that's obvious. What are you doing?" he asked, concern in his blue eyes.

"Huh? Oh, I was looking for Tiger. Couldn't find him."

"Don't worry. I saw him sleeping on a chair in the kitchen by the window. Come over here and sit down." He said gently, as he led her to a chair at the dining table.

"Oh, okay." She muttered, incoherently. The vision still played in front of her eyes. The trench coat, the man, the tattoo, the rain, the letter…

"Adrianna!" Carter said, shaking her.

"What?" she asked, annoyed. She looked up at Carter, to his worried expression. Looking around her, everyone had stopped doing what they were working on, and had turned their attention to her and Carter. "What?" she asked again.

"What happened? Are you alright?" Carter asked. She turned back to him.

"Yeah, I'm fine. Why?"

"Well, you kind of blanked out for a minute there. Are you sure you're alright?"

"Yes." She said. Her eyes widened. "I saw him before."

"Seen who before?" Sam asked, walking over to them.

"The partner, Eddie Miller. I should have realized a long time ago that he had a partner. I was talking to Sara a little bit ago, and she pointed out that I got letters from the Stalker, not the partner, when he was still locked up. Of course, we all assumed that meant he had help on the inside, but we should've realized he needed more help than that. None of the letters were mailed to me! They were all hand delivered and left at my door or in my mailbox. I should have thought of it sooner!" she exclaimed, standing.

She paced along the table, everyone watching her intently. "I saw him! When I was living in Petersburg, I rented a house. I went on a walk around a couple blocks and sat at the park for a bit. But storm clouds started moving in and I could hear thunder in the distance. So, I started heading home."

Sara was coming over that night too, so I was in a rush and trying to beat the storm home. I wasn't paying much attention and ran right into a man walking past me on the sidewalk. When I apologized, he turned to keep walking and I saw it! The tattoo! I didn't think about it then. I was in such a hurry I just ran back to the house. But when I got there, I found another letter. This time it was on the doorstep. He was right there! I should've remembered him! I could've called Alex and ended this all months ago, when the Stalker was still in prison!"

"Adrianna, come sit down. Okay? Please?" Sam urged.

The Adrianna Swift Series
Swift Snake

She looked up from the floor, seeing Sam standing a few feet away, worry wrinkling his dark face. She took a deep stilling breath and willed herself to relax. Sitting back down, Sam sat down next to her while Carter knelt by her side.

"Thank you." He sighed. "Now look, don't blame yourself for not noticing it sooner. We all tend to miss things when we're in a hurry. Our brains are trying to remember everything all the time, and when we're rushing, we just can't remember every little thing."

"Right." Carter added. "I forget crap all the time when I'm rushing out the door, or when I'm late to a meeting or what have you. It's normal."

"I know. But if I had just realized it then, we would've been able to save so much time. Alex could still be alive…" her voice trailed off. She fought back the tears trying to flood her eyes.

"Adrianna…" Garcia quietly replied as she walked over to where she sat. Carter stood up, stretching his legs and back, before leaning against the wall in front of them. The profiler kneeled down in front of Adrianna, starting especially careful so as not to start an argument like she had earlier that day. "You've went through a lot." She gently placed a hand on Adrianna's.

"A majorly traumatic experience. Our brains have the ability to hide certain memories from us. It's part of our brain's defense system. To protect us from anything that can hurt us. At least until we're completely ready to deal with it. Almost everyone has been through something in our lives that, we just don't want to remember. Sometimes, our brains see them as something important, and keep them in our heads all the time. But sometimes, they hide them. In the farthest corners of our minds."

When they do come back to the forefront, it's not because we should feel guilt or resentful, but because it's time for us to process them and go through the motions of dealing with it. You didn't remember until now because you weren't ready to before. But now, you are. That means you're stronger now than you were at that moment. Please, don't blame yourself for that." Her voice ended in a whisper as she watched Adrianna's pained gaze.

"I know you're right," she wiped away a tear that had escaped down her cheek. "But I-."

"No buts. Look, you were meant to remember it now, not then. Just as you were always meant to help us with this case. Don't you believe in fate? I do. Alex came into your life for a reason. Just as he left when he did, for a reason. You were always meant to be here, right now, with all of us. If you had remembered then, maybe we never would have connected all these old cases. The families of all these people, would never have gotten the closure they really need."

Maybe, if you had realized it then, we might have caught the partner, but then they both could've escaped after that and disappeared forever. Maybe they would've hurt more people somewhere else and never been caught and stopped. If you all had stopped the partner and the stalker then, we never would have met you. And frankly, I'm glad we've had the opportunity to meet you. Everything happens for a reason. Sometimes, it really sucks."

Adrianna could see tears welling up in the woman's eyes and squeezed her hand slightly to offer her some sort of comfort. When she spoke again, Adrianna could feel the pain she heard in Garcia's shaky voice. "Sometimes, it's not fair at all. But there's a reason for it. It takes a while to find out what that reason is sometimes, but there is always a reason. Always." She turned her face away and discretely wiped away a tear.

In that moment, Adrianna knew that the woman had been through some sort of heartache like she had, and she felt for her. She wanted to hug her and tell her everything was okay, but she knew it'd draw attention to her tears, and she didn't want to embarrass her. Instead, she held her hand and stroked her palm with her thumb as secretly as possible.

"Thank you." She said, only slightly louder than a whisper. "You're right." She sent her a slight smile and took a deep breath. "You're right. There's no use blaming myself for that when it was always going to happen this way. And I'm glad I've met you too." She straightened in her chair and let go of Garcia's hand. "I'm glad to have met all of you."

Tiger pranced into the room then, as if he didn't want to be left out, and walked over to Adrianna. He stretched and meowed cutely, and then jumped up into her lap. He stood, his face in hers, as he stared at her. He rubbed his face against her cheek and purred as she giggled. "Yes, Tiger. I'm glad to have met you, too. And to be able to take care of you now." He purred even louder in her ear as he placed his feet on her shoulder to get closer for a better nuzzle.

"He's a cutie." Garcia chuckling as she patted his back.

"Yes, he is." Adrianna smiled. "Aren't you? Yes, you're a handsome boy, aren't you Tiger?" Tiger meowed softly and then sat down on her lap soaking up all the attention. Just then, the doorbell rang.

"Oh! I'll get it!" she handed Tiger to Garcia, kissing the top of his head before she wiped away her tears and headed for the front door.

"Wait!" Carter yelled, running up behind her.

She paused by the door, turning. "What?"

"It could be the partner." He said, the Chief and Sam close behind.

"It's dinner. I called in for delivery." She said, ignoring them. She opened the door, smiling at the young man on the doorstep. "Hello!"

"Good evening, ma'am. I have an order for Adrianna Swift."

"Yes, sir. That's me."

"Great. That'll be one hundred and-."

Crack! Boom!

Book 2
Written by N L Hiser

<u>Thirty-One</u>

"**G**et down!" Adrianna grabbed the young man and pushed him to the floor. The food fell around him with a loud thud.

"Adrianna! Get down!"

Crack! Boom!

"Ahh!" she screamed. She threw herself down on top of the man. "Stay down!" she screamed.

Tires squealed as a vehicle sped away down the street. "Adrianna? Are you alright?" Sam yelled, rushing to her side.

"I'm fine! Go after him!" she yelled back. Carter, the Chief, and their people ran out the door.

"Jones stay with Adrianna!" the Chief yelled back.

"Sam!" Iris yelled in fright, as she ran in from the dining room, right on Garcia's heels.

"I'm fine." He stood up and hugged his wife.

"Argh!" the man moaned, as Adrianna slid off him.

"Oh my god." Said the Jones' together.

"Adrianna?" Iris cried.

"I'm fine, Iris. But he's shot. Grab towels. Hurry!" Iris ran to the other room.

"You're going to be okay." She told the man, as Sam called nine-one-one. She put pressure on the wound, causing him to whimper a little. "What's your name?"

"Kyle."

"Kyle? Well, it's nice to meet you Kyle. Don't worry. You're going to be fine. Is there anyone we can call, Kyle?"

"My mom."

"Okay, Kyle. We're going to call your mom. Just stay calm."

"It really hurts." He said, moaning. Adrianna looked at the blood pulling from his shoulder under her hands. She looked at Sam, concerned.

"You're going to be alright, Kyle." Sam said, hanging up the phone. "The ambulance is on the way." He motioned for Adrianna to move her hand and pulled the teens shirt from his shoulder. Looking for a moment, he nodded to Adrianna who continued holding pressure on it. "It's looks like you're a pretty lucky man there, Kyle."

"I don't feel very lucky at the moment." He chuckled softly.

Sam smiled. "Sense of humor, good. You're going to be fine. Just think, you'll have a cool scar to show the girls at your school, and you might even get to be on the news. How's that sound?"

Kyle laughed. "Not bad."

"Good."

Iris returned with towels, and Adrianna and Sam hurriedly used them to wrap Kyles shoulder and soak up blood. Adrianna pulled the towel tight around him, to add extra pressure, and a large ting shot through her arm. "Shit!" she muttered.

"Oh, shit! Adrianna, you're hit." Garcia sat down on the floor beside her.

"Oh, it's alright. It's not that bad." Adrianna tried to brush her off.

"No, stop. We can't have you walking around shot." She took one of the clean towels and tried to wipe away some of the blood. "Sorry." She muttered and then, in an instant, ripped the sleeve from her shirt so the wound was visible. Wiping the blood away as much as she could, she said, "It seems you're pretty lucky tonight, too." She wrapped the towel around Adrianna's arm and tied it tightly in place. "That was a brave thing you did, Adrianna."

"Any one of you would have done the same." She said, letting Sam take over holding pressure on the boys wound.

"Yes, but we're trained for it. We go through so many drills; it becomes our first instinct. *You,* however, are not. You *chose* to protect him."

Adrianna smiled. Then, noticed the food on the floor and turned to Iris. "Hey, will you take all this to the kitchen and put Tiger in my room really fast, so he doesn't get out? Then, will you take this money to KFC to pay for it, please? I don't want any of this to fall back on Kyle here, or for the manager to be short for the night."

"Of course, honey." She answered, smiling. She picked up the food and tucked the money in her pocket before heading to the kitchen.

"Here." Adrianna said, folding up the remainder of the cash she had in her pocket. She tucked it into Kyles pocket. "It's your tip."

He laughed, and then groaned in pain. "Thanks. I hope you enjoy your meal."

Adrianna laughed, "You're a pretty strong kid, you know that?"

"That's what the girls tell me." He winked at her.

Sam laughed, seeing Adrianna blush. "Boy done got shot, and he's sitting here hitting on the ladies." They all laughed.

The Adrianna Swift Series
Swift Snake

Soon, Iris told them she was heading to the restaurant and kissed Sam goodbye. Kissing Adrianna on the forehead, she said, "Take care of yourself, you hear?"

"I will. I'll be here when you get back." Iris jumped in the car and left down the road.

"No, you won't." replied Garcia. "You're going to the hospital. Just like Kyle here."

"No, I'm not. They can fix me up when they get here, but I'm not leaving. Not unless it's to catch this bastard."

"Wait, are you the lady everyone's talking about on the news?" Kyle said, sitting up.

"Yes…" Adrianna answered, hesitantly.

"Cool. You're famous. Did you really shoot that killer?"

"Yes, she did." Garcia interjected.

"That's badass." He smiled.

Adrianna relaxed and smiled. "You're pretty badass, too. I might have to stop by your school to put in a good word for you with the girls."

"Thanks, but I don't really need you to do that. Most of the girls at my school are all superficial and stuff."

Her brow rose. "*Most* of them? So, which one isn't?"

"Becca. Becca O-Reilly. She's awesome."

"Oh. Well, Kyle, Becca would be lucky to date a guy like you."

"Nah. Really?"

She giggled. "Really.

Book 2
Written by N L Hiser

Thirty-Two

Eddie Miller could see the flashing lights in the rearview mirror. They were on him faster than he had expected, and he panicked slightly as he sped away. He couldn't let them catch him.

He tried to remember everything he'd ever learned from watching cop shows. One- be unpredictable or they'll hit you with the spike strip. He quickly turned right and hit the gas. Two- put as much distance between you and the police. As soon as he seen the lights speedily take the right turn, he took a left. Five seconds later he whipped another right. He couldn't see the lights anymore, but he could still hear the sirens wailing.

A moment later he quickly turned left onto a busy street. Three- blend in. He slowed down to the speed limit and made his way down the road as inconspicuously as possible in a stolen car. The sirens still wailed in the distance, but he didn't see them anywhere. He glanced up and down the conjoining streets, as he tried to plan his next step. He stopped at the red light abruptly, cursing himself for drawing unwanted attention. Hs phone slid quickly off the passenger seat and hit the floorboard. Glancing at it aggravated, he leaned over to pick it up, and paused.

He smiled and menacingly with a new thought, and upon seeing the cars in front of him moving again, he swiftly moved to the left lane. A few moments later, he merged onto the exit and got onto the highway. He grinned maliciously and headed out of town.

Thirty-Three

A drianna sat on the back of the ambulance, as one of the paramedics stitched up her arm. Kyle had left in the first ambulance a few moments before, but seemingly in good spirits. The paramedic had assured her before leaving that he would be fine and make a quick recovery. As she sat, the Chief and Carter pulled in to view, and parked their cars. They walked over after they seen Garcia head toward Adrianna.

"Adrianna are you okay?" the Chief asked as he eyed her arm.

"Yeah, I'm fine." She told the paramedic thank you and hopped down. "Did you catch him?" she asked, impatiently.

"No. I'm sorry, Adrianna. We tried, but we lost him."

"Did you get the license plate number?"

"Yes. Stolen from a few streets over, just twenty minutes before he tried to shoot you. Forensics did get some good prints from the scene though, so at least it's something. And every cop on the Island is out looking for him right now. We'll find him."

"Good. At least it's something. Come on." She led them all back into the house, scooting past the forensic uniforms at the door. "What are we doing?"

Iris met them in the hallway. "Eating. Before this food goes to waste."

"But we-." Carter started.

"Are waiting. There isn't much more we can do, just this second, Carter. We might as well eat. We all need it. You've been here since early this morning. And it seems like it's going to be a long night." Garcia added, interrupting Carter.

"True." He agreed as he raked his hands over his face and rubbed his eyes.

"I'll make some coffee." Adrianna said, as she headed for the kitchen.

"No, you don't." Sam stopped her and pulled her down into a chair. "I'll make the coffee. And I'll bring you some water. You've been shot. You need to refuel. Trust me." He disappeared into the kitchen with Iris.

"How are you feeling?" The Chief asked.

"Fine. Tired." She raked her fingers through her short hair.

"You should get some rest."

"Maybe later. After dinner, I need to call and tell Sara what happened though. If I don't, and she sees it on tv, she'll freak out and show up here."

The Chief smiled, tiredly. "Sounds like a good friend."

"She is." She smiled. She thought of how Sara would react but had to shake her head to keep from dozing off.

The Jones' returned from the kitchen, with arms full of food and plates. Sam laid his load on the table and went back, reappearing a moment later with mugs of coffee and bottles of water. They all thanked them and made their plates.

"Thank you for buying dinner, Adrianna." Sam said after a time.

Everyone nodded and thanked her quietly, all too tired to say much of anything. All she could do was smile and nod, before taking the plate Iris handed her. She took a bite which created a triumphant growl from her stomach. It was delicious, and thankfully still plentiful after crashing to the floor. She quickly chugged her bottle of water and ate.

By the time her ravenous appetite was content, she had finished her entire plate and two chocolate chip cookies, still surprisingly warm from the oven, which made her wonder if Iris had reheated everything. Gulping down another bottle of water and halfway through her cup of coffee, she sat back in her chair so full she thought she'd explode. She excused herself and placed her dishes in the sink.

Sipping on her coffee, she sat down at the little table and called Sara. She picked up on the second ring, panic in her voice. "Are you alright?"

"Yes, yes, I'm fine. We had another…incident. I thought I'd better call and let you know before you see it on the news in the morning."

"What happened?"

Sighing and rubbing her stomach, she went on to tell her about all that happened. "Oh my gosh! And to think, you could've been shot. I mean, you were. But shot dead! Are you sure you're okay?"

"Yes, I'm okay." She smiled. "Sore, a little worse for wear, but okay."

"You promise?"

"I promise."

"Good." There was a long pause on the other end, and Adrianna's head slid back against the wall. "Did you all at least get to eat?"

Smiling, she said, "Yep. Just finished. I feel like they could roll me down the hall like a giant bowling ball." She giggled softly.

"That's good. Well," she sighed. "what are you going to do now?" But Adrianna didn't answer. Instead, she heard light, sleepy breathing through the receiver. "Goodnight, Adrianna." She whispered as she giggled softly and ended the call.

Book 2
Written by N L Hiser

Thirty-Four

Adrianna woke up stiff and sore, her arm in pain. She opened her eyes slowly, looking around the kitchen. "Damn. I didn't mean to fall asleep." She muttered to herself. She stood slowly, stretching her back and legs. She tried to stretch her sore arm as well, but the gunshot wound made her arm too stiff and painful to move.

It was dark in the kitchen, except for the small candle burning on the counter. Looking out the window behind her, she could see the sky dark and clear, the stars and moon bright and high in the sky. Remembering what she was doing last, she searched for her phone, finding it on the floor under the chair.

She opened it, seeing the time being almost ten, and quickly texted Sara a sorry for falling asleep on her. When she heard talking in the next room, she wandered in.

"There she is." Sam said as she walked in.

"Hi. I'm sorry I fell asleep. I guess I got full and needed a nap. What'd I miss?"

"I usually do too." The men chuckled. "You didn't miss anything. We've still been waiting and going over everything again for anything we've missed. I would have woken you otherwise."

She sat down at the table, rubbing her eyes. "Honey, maybe you should go to bed for a while. Get a few more hours of sleep. I know you're exhausted." Iris told her from the other side of the table.

"I'm alright. Just stiff and sore. But no more than anyone else here. I know you all are tired too."

"True, but we have to work. You can afford to get some sleep during the boring bits, Adrianna." The Chief retorted.

Sam looked into his wife's weary eyes. "Honey, maybe you both should get some rest. You need it just as much as the rest of us, if not more. I promise, if we hear anything, or if anything at all happens, I'll come wake you both."

"Are you sure?"

"Completely." He smiled, kissing her softly. She held him close and hugged him back tightly.

"Alright. Just for a little while." She stood and walked over to Adrianna. "Come on."

"I'm-." She sighed in defeat and nodded as she stood. "I could use a shower at least. And give Tiger some attention, too."

Iris grinned and walked with her out of the room. Her phone vibrated in her pocket. Taking it out, she smiled at the text Sara had sent her, telling her it was okay and goodnight. As she followed Iris up the stairs, she glanced back to the dining room. Garcia stood in the doorway, watching. This time, she didn't feel annoyed or guarded. Instead, she only felt warmth toward the woman, and knew she was only watching because she wanted to make sure she was okay.

She got to her room and opened the door to see Tiger asleep on the bed. "Hold on." Iris said, before striding into her room. A second later, she returned and handed Adrianna a bottle of ibuprophen. "It'll help with the soreness and pain. No more than two though. You don't want it the thin the blood too much and your wound to start seeping."

"Thanks, Iris."

"You're welcome, honey."

"Get you some sleep. I'll see you in a few."

"You, too." She said, sighing. She walked away into her bedroom, leaving Adrianna in the hall. Adrianna smiled tiredly and went into her room as well.

Closing the door behind her, she made her way to the bed and collapsed onto it. Tiger meowed in contempt and rolled over. Her arm hurt badly, pain throbbing throughout. From her elbow to her shoulder, pain rang and vibrated through the tissue. Knowing no veins or arteries were nicked, and that the bullet never hit the bone, she knew it was just the stiffness that made it radiate so.

She sat up, finding her water bottle from the night before, still sitting on her nightstand. Leaning over, she grabbed it and took the ibuprophen Iris had given her. Tired still, she stood and went to the bathroom. Deciding a hot bath would relieve her achy body better, she plugged the tub and started the water.

She meandered back to the room and dropped her clothes on the chair beside the bed. Petting Tiger, she returned to the bathroom and added lavender bath bubbles to the running water. Smiling as she remembered Iris telling her that they had been using the room as a guest room since the kids moved out, she knew Iris had put the lavender bath bubbles in the restroom as an added touch to help relax her guests.

"She really does think of everything." She uttered to herself amid the noise of the water.

The water rose fairly quickly as she brought her laptop in and started some music. Being careful not to have it too loud for Iris down the hall, she then turned off the faucet and slid into the hot water. Leaning back against the cool porcelain, she shivered and lowered herself farther into the depth, being careful not to let her bandages hit the water. She breathed in the lavender aroma and closed her eyes.

The Adrianna Swift Series
Swift Snake

Her shoulders fell, breathing slowed, muscles loosened up, and her mind calmed. She slowly dipped her head farther into the water, soaking her hair. Raising up, she shampooed and conditioned, before leaning back again.

She found her loofa floating between her calves and added soap to it. Lathering herself, gently and careful not to get her arm, she then sat back and relaxed against the wall of the tub. Using the loofa to rinse herself, she took her time and enjoyed it. After then rinsing her hair again, she sat back and let the water warm her.

She found herself drifting off a while later, so she unplugged the tub and stood. Grasping the warm towel from its heater, she gently squeezed the extra moisture from her hair and wrapped the towel around her body. Stepping from the tub, she was careful not to leave a trail of water as she walked over to the mirror.

She wiped the condensation from the mirror and gazed at herself. Her eyes were still a little red and swollen from the long day she's had and all the tears she had shed. Feeling the light, barely visible scar along her cheek, she smiled, happy that it was hard for anyone to see.

Her hand grasped the corner of the towel and pulled it open. Staring at her naked body in her reflection, she ran her eyes over her body and the scars that lined it. The Stalker had left his mark, and now she knew the partner probably had as well.

Her eyes roved over the longest scar, running from right below her left hip to the top of her rib cage on her right side. It had healed nicely, considering, but was still as wide as a pencil for most of the length. If he had wanted to, he needed only press his blade into her skin harder, and he would have cut her wide open. Instead, it was no more than a quarter inch deep. There's no fixing that, she thought. No way to make the scars disappear.

She remembered how it had felt when Alex touched her, and how he had kissed her scar, making her mind forget she even had one, even if only for a few moments. She tried to smile at herself in the mirror, trying to reassure herself of the same feeling he had once given her. The feeling that she was still beautiful. It's a petty thing, she knew. But every woman wishes to feel beautiful. She did once, but it was going to take a long time for her to feel that way again. If ever again.

The Adrianna Swift Series
Swift Snake

She wrapped the towel around her and walked back into the bedroom. She pulled on a comfortable outfit, turned off the music, and brought her computer back to the room, before shutting it off for the night. She plugged up her phone and checked that Tiger still had food and water before turning off the lights and sliding under the covers. Tiger meowed and stood up to stretch.

"Hey, baby boy." She whispered. He sidled up to her and stood on her chest. Purring in her ear as she stroked his back, he patty-caked on her shirt. "Ouch! Easy, Tiger. You can't be clawing me." She giggled. He nuzzled against her cheek, purring loudly. Then laid down on, rolled over, and exposed his stomach. Rubbing his belly, she chuckled as he purred and meowed, talking to her. She smiled as he reached out his paw and touched her face, gently holding his bean toes on her. "You're so cute." she murmured.

She laid her hand over his little belly, as he relaxed his arm back to the blanket, and kissed his forehead. She picked him up and laid him beside her, scooting herself farther under the blankets. She laid on her side facing him, as he yawned and stretched. Stepping over closer, he laid down against her and buried his head in her chest. Yawning around a content smile, she rested her bandaged arm on top of the blanket and drifted off to sleep.

Book 2
Written by N L Hiser

Thirty-Five

S he sleepily rolled over but stopped midway when she realized she couldn't move. She opened her eyes and looked at her hands in confusion.

Instead of being in her bed at the Jones' house, she was on the metal table again. In the warehouse! She panicked and tried to pull her hands from the handcuffs but only clanked painfully. She jerked her feet but couldn't break free of the straps.

"No!" She couldn't get free.

"Hello, Katherine."

She looked over towards the voice in the dark. His voice! The Stalker!

"No!" She screamed. He smirked and moved closer with his knife.

"Let me have a turn with this one, man. This one's feisty." The slimy partner, Edward Miller, sneered grotesquely as he stepped toward her.

"Together." The Stalker smiled.

Her eyes widened in fear and panic. "No-no! Please, no! Not again! I killed you! No!" She screamed. They moved closer, closer, and closer until she could feel their sweaty hands and cold metal of the blade against her. "No!"

She jerked against her confines and screamed in pain, as her arm tinged. Her eyes snapped open in realization and found herself back in her bed. She panted and searched her arm. A small scratch from Tiger's claw etched in red laid on her skin. She breathed a sigh of relief and tried to calm herself. Tiger stood at the bottom of her bed, scared. Her jerking had frightened him.

She sat back against the pillows, and slowly drifted back to sleep as her breathing relaxed.

Thirty-Six

He sat in the black truck, smoke **from** his cigarette rolling out of the cracked window. He gulped down the last of his beer, chucking it into the backseat. Belching loudly, he took another drag.

Taking a large swig, beer running down is chin, he reclined back in his seat and sighed happily. He flicked his cigarette out the window, reaching for another to light up. The flame shown on his eyes, making them seem ablaze. He clicked his lighter off, tossing it in the seat as well.

Suddenly, a car drove past. He ducked down and rolled up his window further, watching it disappear around the curve. "Hmm, maybe it's time I find myself a bed for the night instead of staying in the car." He snickered, taking another drag from his cigarette. The cherry burned red hot as he pulled, inhaling half the tobacco stick at once.

Blowing it out of the window, he sat up and turned over the ignition.

He turned down the road, driving for a few minutes before eyeing a house for sell a few streets over. He smirked to himself. "Well now, this will work just fine." He drove up to the house, parking across the road as if he were just another vehicle for a neighboring house. Field dressing his cigarette, he tossed it to the side and walked across the street. With his jacket's collar up, he headed around to the back of the house. Jimmying the lock, he let himself in.

Thirty-Seven

She ran through the woods, weaving between the trees. The light was rapidly dimming as the sun sank over the mountain, creating wild shadows playing along the ground. She felt the moisture in the air stick to her cheeks as she ran. Her chest heaved as her breathe came hard and fast, the cold showing as a cloud escaping her.

Her feet pounded the ground, her ankles taking the weight as she traversed the rugged terrain under her. Sweat stuck her shirt to her skin, but she ignored it all. She ran with all her might, pushing herself to go farther and faster.

She smiled as she seen the familiar creek come into view, the water ran gently as the cold tried to freeze it. Slowing to a slight jog until she reached the creek, she stopped right beside it, enjoying the sound.

She loved living so close to a creek. She remembered all the times spent by the river as a child, fondly. Being by the water and the woods were her true happy place in life. Even on her most stressful day, sitting by the water, totally secluded from life's chaotic events, she could get out of her own head and just breathe.

She sat down on a boulder and closed her eyes and took a deep steadying breath. Listening to the songs of birds in the trees around her, calming her heart, she appreciated the tranquility of it all. Smiling, she focused her senses on all that was around her.

Craning her ears to listen to the scurrying of squirrels across the frosted leaves along the floor of the woods. She could hear them jump from branch to branch, hiding their treasures in their homes. The sound of a woodpecker could be heard in a tree, no more than twenty yards away.

Birds swooped here and there, either preparing to leave for the winter or securing their nests for the hard months ahead. She opened her eyes slowly, gazing at the beauty around her. The water glided over the rocks in front of her, gurgling and splashing, reminding her of the wonder of nature.

The distinct sound of a footfall landed on dry leaves somewhere close, catching her attention. Moving very slowly, she slid off the boulder and crouched low to the ground. Hearing another small step, she craned her eyes into the distance to spot movement. A deer stood behind a thorn bush twenty yards away, watching her. She smiled, her heart easing back to its regular rhythm. The doe seemed to relax as well as she continued to chew on the grass.

She sat in the grass, happy to be home. A feeling of contentment, one she hadn't felt in an awfully long time, welled up inside her. The feeling warmed her as she closed her eyes, taking a relaxing breath of fresh air.

Deciding to go back to the house, she stood slowly, trying her best not to spook the doe or any other creature around. She strolled back to the edge of the woods, eyeing the small house in the distance. She stepped out from the trees into the clearing, when suddenly all the color was drained from her sight like the rush of a waterfall.

The clearing, house, and everything else vanished. Instead, she was back in the Jones' house. Standing on the other side of her room, looking over at the body laying asleep in her bed. She tried to ask who was in her bed, but the only sound that left her lips was a menacing laugh, making her involuntarily cringe.

Feeling a weight in her hand, she raised it closer to her face to see better in the dark. A long butcher knife was clasped in fingers, dirty and scarred. Confused, she glanced at her reflection in the window.

"Ah!" she screamed and bolted out of bed. She looked around the dark room, but it was empty except for herself and Tiger. She looked at her hands. The knife was gone and so was the fingers she seen grasp it a moment ago. It was just a dream. She sighed, remembering how it felt to be back home. "Soon." She whispered.

She walked over to the window, searching for anything abnormal outside. Everything looked the same as when she went to sleep hours ago, but a feeling of unease followed her as she laid back in bed. Tiger crawled onto her lap, helping slightly as he demanded attention. Snuggled up with Tiger, she felt better.

Two horrible nightmares in one night. She was exhausted and her arm was still sore. She looked around the room anxiously. She wasn't sure she wanted to go back to sleep.

.

Book 2
Written by N L Hiser

Thirty-Eight

When she got up a couple of **hours** later, she was still fighting a feeling of unease. Adrianna tried to tell herself it was just because she had a weird dream about him being in her room, watching her sleep, but it didn't help. It felt like something was coming- or was already there. And finding herself back on that table had left an uncontrollable panic in her heart. She was worried it would turn into a panic attack.

"Adrianna?"

"Hmm?" she jerked herself back to reality.

"Are you alright?"

"Yeah." The questioning look was etched deeply into Iris's face. She shook herself physically, noting how everyone around her was now focused on her. "I'm sorry. I'm having a hard time focusing today, I guess."

"How did you sleep?" Sam asked.

"As well as might be expected, I guess."

"Any more nightmares?" Iris asked quietly.

"Yeah, but they'll go away eventually. It just left me a little uneasy is all."

"Uneasy?" Sam questioned.

"Yeah. It turned into sort of a weird out of body thing. Like I was him but standing in my room watching me sleep. It was just, weird. Now, I just can't shake the uneasy feeling. Just one of those dreams that stick with you all day I guess." She could see them exchange looks of concern. "But I'm fine."

Garcia leaned forward. "Uneasy like you're being watched?"

"No…more like someone's coming. Kind of like when you know a relative is on their way but it's one that you don't get along with and you dread their arrival."

"Hmmm." Garcia sat back, pondering. "Maybe it's just because you know what's coming."

"Exactly. That's all it is."

"That, and you probably need more sleep." Iris added.

"Yeah, probably. So, do all of you, though. As soon as we're done with this, we can all get some much-needed rest. Until then, let's get some work done." She retorted. No one tried to argue with her after that. Too tired for the added stress, she was glad the subject was dropped.

The day went past much like the days before. Searching for an answer that would help lead them to capturing Eddie Miller and ending the whole ideal, but not really finding much. By lunch, her eyes were tired and sore from reading over and over the many files, trying to find something, anything, that could help them.

She was sipping on yet another cup of coffee when Agent Carter got a call. Excitement clearly beamed from him as he ended the call and turned to the room. "We just got a match!"

"Really?" Adrianna exclaimed.

He nodded, smiling from ear to ear. "They found some camera footage from a zoo. It was years ago, but they were able to clean it up. Ninety percent match for the Stalker."

"At a zoo?" the Chief asked.

"Yes. Apparently, they worked there together. It could very possibly be how they met. We've already contacted the zoo and got the information sent to us. It'll be faxed from the department any minute." He added, nodding to Sam. Sam nodded and rushed to his office to retrieve the papers. "Get this, Adrianna. The Stalker and Edward Miller worked in the herpetarium."

"Sorry? What's a herpetarium?"

"The reptile pavilion in a zoo." He answered. "They both were in charge of the entire reptile and amphibian section. And their boss, he said Miller was always talking about spiders and snakes, and how amazing he thought they were. The two of them were seen as odd and sometimes creepy by other employees, so they were almost always together. A couple of the employees added that they often arrived and left together because

Miller didn't have a home and was staying with the Stalker."

Sam came back in the room with the papers. "It says here, the Stalker's name is Randal Wright."

"We finally have his name." Adrianna breathed.

"Yes. And now, we have his history. And an old address. The zoo was here, at their start. It was years ago, but we can still go check it out."

"Then what are we waiting for?" Adrianna asked, excitedly standing.

Everyone smiled. They finally had a good breakthrough. Finally, some answers. They all got their things together and headed out of the house, Iris at the door waving them off. "Please be careful!" she yelled, as the cars revved up and started down the street.

Book 2
Written by N L Hiser

<u>Thirty-Nine</u>

Her excitement welled up inside **her**, as she fidgeted in her seat while the car rolled through town. Since she could do nothing but wait until they arrived, she texted Sara to let her know everything that was going on. After a few minutes, Sara replied just as excited as her and telling Adrianna to be careful and to call her when they left.

The caravan of vehicles made its way through the island, like a large worm through the dirt. They ended at the other end of Staten Island, where more dilapidated buildings sat, abandoned, and scheduled for demolition. Finally, they pulled up to a three-story apartment building. It looked run down, but Agent Carter said the owner had scheduled remodeling to begin next week.

"There may not be anything left to find, Adrianna. So, don't get your hopes up. But we could get lucky. The owner cleared everyone out of the building last month and is currently cleaning everything out for the remodel." Carter mentioned as she got out of the car and joined him and the others on the sidewalk. "Luckily for us, the owner has given us permission to come in and search walls and all. Saves us time now that we don't need a warrant."

"Well, that's good news." The Chief replied. "Now, come on. Let's go dig up some dirt on this guy." His voice rang as if ordering his troops into battle. They all quickly went inside and retrieved the keys from the owner, as everyone made their way up the steps to apartment seventeen.

The door clicked open, and a stale stench whooshed passed them as they entered the apartment. The Chief, Sam, and Agent Carter entered first, making sure everything was safe. Adrianna didn't mind. She really wasn't wanting any unexpected craziness today. Plus, her arm was still fairly sore. Just a moment later, they heard the 'all clear' and went inside. They all put on gloves and checked each room.

It looked as if no one had lived there for a decade or more. Dust stuck to all the surfaces nearly an inch deep. The carpet was heavily soiled with dirt, ash, food remnants, and what Adrianna was certain was crap.

Careful not to touch anything, she made her way toward the bedroom. In the doorway, she paused and whipped around when she heard Garcia shriek. She turned just in time to see the largest rat she had ever seen, jump out of one of the kitchen cabinets Garcia had just opened and land by her foot, running away and causing everyone to dodge out of its way.

Everyone kind of laughed as Garcia straightened herself, yet Adrianna could see everyone glancing here and there apprehensively, afraid of another rat running out from the filth.

She walked into the bedroom. By one wall laid a mattress on the floor, stained and smelling. There was no other furniture left in the apartment as far as Adrianna could tell. Sam stood searching the dark closet in the corner, as the Chief and Carter stood by the mattress contemplating. Curious, Adrianna walked over to them.

"What are you doing?"

"We checked the rest of the room. Only other place to check is under here."

"Good luck with that." She laughed, backing away. "I ain't touching that thing."

"You don't want to do it?" Sam snickered jokingly as he walked over to her.

"Hell no! Who knows what's on that thing." She answered seriously.

They laughed but finally decided that they'd lift the mattress while Adrianna and Sam would grab anything under it. Carter and the Chief lifted the disgusting old mattress, revealing a photo album and a trinket box. A used syringe lay beside them, rusted.

"Be careful not to touch the syringe, Adrianna."

"I got it." Sam moved it out of the way so it wouldn't prick anyone. They gently picked up the items and backed out of the way, so the guys could lower the mattress back down.

Adrianna carefully opened the album to the first page, horror filling her. "Oh my god!" she gasped.

"What is it?" Sam asked. The men moved closer to look. "Oh my god."

There on the first page was a photo of a woman, tied and gagged, and obviously dead. Below that was two more. Their names were written above each picture, with a note of where they got her and the date.

"Here." The Chief said. He opened a large evidence bag and they gently placed the album inside and sealed it.

Sam opened the trinket box and paused, showing them the contents. Wedding rings. A lot of wedding rings. And snips of hair. They had found their souvenirs. Carefully placing the box and its contents in another evidence bag, they sealed it. They joined the others in the living room, showing them what they had found. Everything searched, they decided to leave.

As Sam headed out of the door, another giant rat, or perhaps the same one, ran past his foot, causing him to bump the door. The door swung slightly closed behind him, and Adrianna caught a glance of something on the inside of the door. Pulling it farther closed, Garcia walked up beside her.

"What is it?"

There on the back of the door was a picture of Adrianna and beside it, a photo of her and Sara. Knives had been thrown at them like darts, still stuck in the door. Eddie Miller had been there more recently than they thought.

"Who is that?" Garcia asked.

"Sara." Adrianna whispered, frightened. "Does this mean she's next?"

"I-I don't know." Garcia gently pulled the photos from the door and stuck them and the knives in evidence. Adrianna ran out of the door. "Adrianna!" Garcia yelled, but she was already gone.

<u>Forty</u>

Please pick up! Please pick up! Please pick up!" She muttered to herself as she frantically called Sara.

"Adrianna, I'm sure she's alright. You just talked to her before we got here." Sam said as the car sped down the road. Garcia sat beside her, trying to calm her.

The phone stopped ringing and ended the call. "Damn!" she yelled. She immediately looked through her contacts and found Sara's dads house number and dialed. He picked up on the second ring. "Oh, thank god! Hey, this is Adrianna. Is Sara there?"

"Oh hey, Adrianna. No, she's not. Her tires were slashed this afternoon while she was at the gym. She's at the garage now getting new one's put on. Is everything alright?"

"No! She's not answering her phone. Call the garage. Tell them to not let her leave and get there to her as soon as you can. She's in danger! I can't explain now. I'm on my way!" she hurried and hung up the phone. She tried to call Sara's phone again, but still no answer.

"Adrianna?" Garcia urged.

"Her tires were slashed a little bit ago. She's supposed to be at the garage but she's not picking up her phone."

"Look, we don't know that anything's wrong. She could just be busy talking to the guys at the garage. We can't just rush down there. Try and call her again."

Adrianna dialed again, this time it was picked up on the first ring. "Oh, thank god!"

"Hello, Katherine…" her heart sunk, as she recognized the voice on the other end. She put the phone on speaker.

"Miller, if you hurt her…"

"Oh? You'll do what exactly?"

"I *will* find you, asshole. And I *will* kill you." Everyone in the car was silent and listening as they whirled through traffic back towards the house.

"Oh? Is that right? Because I'm pretty sure Sara here is the one going to die."

"Adrianna! Help!" Sara's scream rang through the phone.

"Sara! I'm coming! I promise, I'm coming!" Adrianna cried.

Sara's voice was again muffled as Miller continued. "Now, what are you going to do, *Katherine*?"

"I'm coming. I'm going to hunt you down and kill you. Just like I killed your little friend." She bit out, little more than a whisper.

He was silent, and Adrianna knew he was fuming. But she knew better than to push too far. Sara wouldn't last long enough for her to get to her if she did. Finally, he hissed, "We'll be waiting." And hung up.

Carter sat in the front seat, listening. "Adrianna-."

"You take me, or I go by myself!" she snapped. She looked at them, daring them to go against her.

They silently nodded, and Sam punched the gas, lurching them forward. They made it to the house within ten minutes. They explained what happened to Iris and even though she didn't want her or Sam to go, she never tried to stop them. She agreed to watch Tiger for Adrianna and waved them goodbye five minutes later as they all piled into the SUV to leave. She gave Sam a kiss and hug. Then he climbed in with the others. A minute later, they were on the road to Petersburg.

Adrianna waved goodbye to Iris as they drove away, her worried expression sending a ping of guilt into Adrianna's gut. She sat back against the seat, sorry for dragging Sam away from her. It was out of Sam's jurisdiction. He was only going to be a friend and help Adrianna. She didn't think Carter would've let him come along otherwise.

Glancing up to the rearview mirror, Sam's eyes were sad and twisted in concern. She forced herself to look away and watched out the window as the houses and cars passed by.

The people went on with their day, unknowing what was about to happen. She wished life were that simple again. Like back before that night, when she had no other concerns than what immediately affected her and her family and friends. Back when she didn't pay any attention to the chaos the news showed on the television.

She knew that bad things were happening in other places, but like most of the people she knew, she never thought those things would ever happen to her or someone she knew. Being oblivious is bliss, apparently, she thought as she watched children play in the park as they drove by.

Barely thirty minutes after hitting the road, Sara's dad called. He had made it to the garage, but Sara wasn't there. There was a bloody wrench, but no Sara. Adrianna spent the next few minutes explaining what was going on and trying to calm him down. He was hysterical over his daughter, as any parent would be. Finally, she convinced him to go to the police station.

Garcia called the local police chief and filled them in on what was happening. It was an FBI case, so he took over via phone and had everything in motion for when they arrived. He had the chief plan for an officer to keep Sara's dad company, while he waited. Everything was ready for them to get there, but they were still hours away.

Unable to commission a ride via helicopter or plane, their only option was to drive as quickly as possible. The local officers would hold their positions until they got to town and not try to take him down themselves. It could jeopardize Sara's life if they tried and if Miller insisted on seeing Adrianna. They apparently hated it, but Garcia assured Adrianna that they wouldn't move until Carter's order.

After a while, she talked to Sara's dad, hearing him slightly calmer. She promised to check in with him frequently and promised she would get Sara back safe. She could hear his voice shake as they talked, but there was nothing else she could do for him at the moment. All any of them could do was wait until they reached town.

As they sped to Petersburg, and Sara, she listened as the others discussed what was going to happen when they arrived. They had a plan, but she had her own plan. She knew he wouldn't make it easy for them to find him, and she knew Sara could die before they even reached her town, much less find her. It was going to be hours before they even got there. Anything could happen. But she knew what she needed to do. The hard part was going to be waiting until they got there.

It was going to be a long few hours, she complained silently. She pulled her backpack into her lap and held it close. Just knowing what she had hidden away inside was enough to comfort her a little. She closed her eyes from the sights of the world outside her window and let the other's voices guide her off to sleep. Now was the time to rest up for what was to come.

Book 2
Written by N L Hiser

<u>Forty-One</u>

S he woke every so often when the car would hit a bump and jar her awake, hurting her arm. She'd listen to the conversation going on around her, making sure she didn't miss anything new, and then drift off to sleep again. She did her best to not let the others know she had woken and to get as much rest as she could. She knew she was going to need it.

The partner, Miller, wasn't as smart as Randal Wright was, but it would be stupid to underestimate him. Even after Wright had died, he had made it this long without being caught and had managed to break into the Jones' house, and managed to shoot Adrianna and the delivery guy, Kyle. All without getting caught. And now he had made it out of state and kidnaped Sara and was holding her somewhere. He was smart enough, and that made him dangerous. But this time, Adrianna was bringing back up from the FBI as well. No matter what, she vowed to herself, he doesn't get away, and he doesn't get to hurt Sara. No matter what.

Finally, she recognized a sign and realized they were only an hour away. She quickly texted Sara's dad to let him know when they'd be there. They had made good time. Thankful, she watched out of the window at the passing trees and tried to calm her anticipation. She had only felt it so strong once before, and that was when she was waiting for Wright to reveal himself on her property. The waiting before the fight, it was nearly unbearable.

As she sat in silence, fighting the urge to demand Sam drive faster, she thought of her times with Sara. She was the most genuine friend she had had in years, perhaps since childhood. Sara was one of the only people she had confided in about…everything. After she had seen the letter that night, she had told her about her family, The Stalker, the letters, the nightmares, and her panic attacks. Even now, she knew Sara was one of the only people that could calm her down during an attack.

She remembered that night, how Sara had held her close and whispered to her. How she stayed the nightmares that had again creeped into her dreams. How she never judged her or showed pity towards her. Instead, she never failed to tell her the truth and showed her what she was truly capable off.

Before that night, Adrianna had felt as if she was broken. She felt like the Stalker had taken her life, just as if she had never left that warehouse alive. He permanently fucked her and made her feel as if she could never recover. Forever broken and defeated. Sara changed that. Sara changed her, and she knew it. Without Sara, she knew she wouldn't have made it this far. He probably would've found her and did exactly what he promised he would. Without Sara, she knew, she would've died.

She changed me, she thought, fighting the tears that threatened to fall. She's the only reason I've made it this far and survived. Because of her, I'm stronger. Physically and mentally. I won't let her die. I won't! She vowed to herself. No matter the cost. She gave me my life back. I won't let him take hers from her. He will not win. I ended Randal Wright. It's time I end his partner, Edward Miller, too.

The Adrianna Swift Series
Swift Snake

She closed her eyes, drawing every memory of Sara and their conversations to her forethought. This time, she wasn't just fighting for revenge. This time, she was fighting for her friend's life. And this time, she thought, I won't make the mistake of letting him get the upper hand. No, this time, I'm going to end it once and for all. This time, I won't go in headfirst. Instead, I'm going to be smarter than who I'm fighting. Because I have something worth so much more than revenge, that I'm fighting for. It's time to end this, for good this time.

Forty-Two

When they pulled up to the police station a half hour later, they all piled out of the SUV and greeted the local police Chief at the door. Adrianna left her backpack in the car, where she knew no one would bother messing with it. She walked inside and headed to the bathroom with Garcia to relieve themselves. Throwing some water on her face as she washed her hands, she stared at herself in the mirror, determination in her eyes. Garcia slightly squeezed her shoulder, watching her. Adrianna just dried herself and nodded, following her from the room.

Sara's dad met her in the hallway. Before she had a moment to say anything at all, he grabbed her and pulled her into a strong hug, collapsing into uncontrollable sobs. She held him close, trying to comfort him as well as she could. Finally, he relaxed a little and let go of her, wiping away his tears.

"I'm so glad you're here, Adrianna. It's nice to see you again." He laughed nervously. "You shouldn't have come though. There's nothing you can do. The cops still haven't found her."

"We will." Adrianna insisted.

"But I don't understand. How are you even involved in this? Who is this man that took my-my..." he cried; his wall of solidity collapsed once again.

"He doesn't know?" Garcia asked, confused.

"Doesn't know what?" he urged.

"Come sit down. I'll explain everything."

Adrianna took his hand and helped him sit down in a chair down the hall. She told him about the murder of her family, how she had been taken and then rescued. She told him how her and his daughter had met, and how after beating Wright, they had found out he had a partner all along. She told him everything he needed to know but made sure not to include anything that would make the current situation much harder on him.

"Did Sara know all this?" he stared at her.

"Yes. I told her everything. She was there one night when I was doing pretty bad. She kind of coaxed it out of me." She smiled. "She's my rock. She's the only reason I've made it this far."

He sat in silence, pondering. "So…you're here to get revenge?"

"No." She answered quickly. "I'm here to get Sara back and to make sure this bastard never hurts anyone ever again." She squeezed his hand in hers, looking him in the eye. "I promise you. I'm going to get Sara back."

He nodded silently. Sam walked up to them and cleared his throat. She squeezed his hand again and smiled slightly, trying to offer some sort of reassurance.

"I have to go. I'll be back soon. Stay here." She whispered to the man. Standing and walking over to Sam, "What's up?" she asked quietly.

"The locals have searched all over town. No one has found any sign of either one of them. We need to regroup."

"Alright, let's get to it." she glanced back at Sara's dad, silently hoping for a miracle, before following Sam.

They met up with everyone in one of the few conference rooms, all the bustling around grinded to a halt as Adrianna closed the door behind her. "Adrianna, this is the police chief, Malony."

Shaking his hand, "Nice to meet you, Chief."

Malony nodded. "I have to say, this is a new one to me. I mean, we've never had a victim in such a position to help us catch the guy before."

She smiled politely, knowing well that he meant that he wasn't keen to the way they were doing things. "Well, maybe Sir, that's exactly why this is going to work." The Chief looked slightly taken aback, and a sudden rush of accomplishment filled Adrianna. "Okay, let's get to work. I assume everyone's up to speed on the case?" Everyone in the room nodded or murmured in agreement. "Good. So, where haven't you looked?" Silence filled the small, crowded room. Looking around she continued. "Okay… was there anything left behind at the garage? Or any clue as to where they were heading?"

"The only thing that was left at the garage was her purse and a bloody wrench. It wasn't a lot of blood, so he may have used it to knock her out. No fingerprints, no forensics at all." One of the officers replied.

"Okay, how about Sara's phone. He answered it. Maybe he still has it. Can we get a location on it?"

"The GPS is turned off on it." Sam replied.

"Have you tried calling it?" Garcia asked Malony.

"No. You told us not to contact him in any way, but to just try to find the woman." The police chief answered, obvious aggravation on his face.

"Her names Sara!" Adrianna bit out, angrily. "It probably wouldn't have been a good idea. If you call and I'm not the one he's speaking to, if he answers at all, he could get pissed and kill Sara." Adrianna glanced around the room at all the pages being pinned on the board and scattered along the table. "Hmmm, does anyone have a map?"

"A map?" an officer asked from beside her.

"Yeah. Of the town and it's outskirts. Every building and house?"

"Yeah, I can get you one. Hold on." He ran out of the room. He quickly returned with the large map and helped Adrianna spread it over the table.

She quietly scanned each section, running her fingers over the illustrations of landmarks. "What are you thinking?" Garcia asked over her shoulder. Everyone stepped closer, looking over the paper.

"Where would he go?" Adrianna answered just over a whisper. Almost muttering to herself. "Where would he take her?" Her eyes darted around the map like a young dancer trying to nail every step.

"We've searched the entire town." A deputy chimed in. "We've even called or checked on every house inside of town. The only ones left are-."

"On the outskirts." Garcia added pointedly.

"There!" Adrianna exclaimed, jabbing a finger at a building on the map. "What is that?"

Looking at where she was pointing, Garcia glanced to the police Chief. One of the deputies answered instead, "That was the old mill, but it's been shut down for a while. Maybe four or five years now, I think. Not much left but an old shell of the building and dust now."

"That's where he's at." Adrianna said.

"Why there?"

"It's the type of place they like. They prefer old, abandoned places covered in dust and filth. I guess they think it's the last place anyone would go looking for them or run into them by accident. Is there any power to the building?" Garcia answered.

"Shouldn't be."

"Call the power company. See if any power source seems to be draining any energy there. If so, call us. I'll need them to turn off all power in that area, but not until I say. If we go too soon, he could get jumpy." Carter ordered.

"Yes, sir." The officer replied and left the room.

"Come on." Adrianna urged. She left the room and headed for the front doors.

They quickly followed her. "Wait! Adrianna, we can't go in there all gun-hoe! We need a plan!" Carter yelled.

"Then get to work. You can come up with your plan in the car. We have to move now! He's not going to wait forever. We're running out of time. We need to move now!"

The team glanced at one another, grabbed their things, and rushed out the door behind her. She quickly jumped in the back of the SUV and strapped in, grabbing her backpack. Everyone clambered in with her. A moment later, a convoy of FBI and police vehicles were rushing to the abandoned mill.

Forty-Three

"O kay. Let's hear it. What's the plan?" Adrianna asked Carter.

He looked at the map. "Alright. It looks like there's forest around most of the mill. Streets on one side of it, but they look to be residential. We'll have teams stationed around the building in case he tries to escape, and then two teams flanking the front. We'll move in, slowly and quietly. The longer we go undetected, the better your friend's chances. If there's power, we'll have them cut it after we enter the building. Maybe we'll get lucky and it'll draw him away from your friend to try to get the power back. That'll be our best shot at taking him down."

"Okay. What's plan B?"

"Plan B is we find another way of getting him away from your friend and detain him while we secure her safety."

"That's it?"

"Well…yeah. You're expecting something else?"

"No…just a little more plan to it. I mean, you are the FBI." Adrianna teased.

"Well you've given me all of five minutes to come up with a good plan that won't get us all killed and won't let him escape."

"I know. But you did good." She joked. "You know I'm going in with you." It was a statement. He knew there was no talking her out of it. She was determined and ready to win the argument she was sure was coming. They both knew she'd go in anyways, no matter what he said.

"Okay, but you do what we say. And you stay behind me and Agent Garcia. Got it?"

"Got it." She knew that this was their jobs, their lives. Not just hers. Not just Sara's. She was glad there wasn't an argument. She didn't want to put anyone in danger. No slip ups this time. No. No slip ups. This time, he goes to prison. This time, no one dies.

Book 2
Written by N L Hiser

They reached the street that lead to the old mill and pull the cars over to the side of the road. They could see the mill, or what was left of it, about five hundred yards ahead. Chief Malony called in to the station while Carter reiterated to the rest of the group the game plan. Half of the convoy split off to other streets. They would park farther down the road and go in on foot to surround the back of the building, using the forest to cover their pursuit. The deputy back at the station had contacted the power company. A small source was found on what looked like the second floor. Malony told the deputy to stand by with the company, ready for their order. They slowly and quietly coasted their cars into position, a mere thirty yards from the front doors.

Adrianna slid her hand into her bag as everyone stepped out of the vehicles. She stepped down onto the road, and carefully attached her holster to her hip. Seeing her do so, the team shook their heads at her. Refusing silently, she positioned herself behind them and insisted they move on.

"Fine. Don't unholster it unless you have to. Everyone stay as quiet as possible. If he hasn't noticed us outside yet, let's keep it that way. Adrianna, watch yourself. Follow us and watch our backs." Adrianna nodded in agreement. "Let's move." Carter whispered.

They moved stealthily toward the doors, Adrianna following close on their heels. As one of the team gently eased one of the doors open a crack, it began to creak loudly. Glancing over his shoulder, Carter gave Garcia the signal. She quickly radioed the deputy and gave the order to cut off the power. Two seconds later, they swiftly entered the building as an electrical whirring slowed to a stop. Adrianna propped the door open behind them with a nearby rock.

They entered a long dark hallway, the floor covered in a few inches of dust except for a single trail of footprints. Feeling a slight relief and anticipation at knowing she had chosen the right place, she calmed herself and followed the rest of the group. The air was hard to breath. Thick from sawdust, and heavy from the heat outside, her lungs ached. It took every fiber of stubbornness in her not to cough. Each step that kicked up the loose particles only made it worse.

At the end of the hallway, it turned the corner. Light penetrated the room from the many windows lining the walls. Though covered like everything else, sunlight still broke through moderately. To their right was an open room, one she presumed was where the workers would clock in and stash away their lunch pails and things since there were some lockers left behind. Beside the snack machines and water tank, a sign hung crooked on the wall that read: Restroom.

Past the room, pallets lined the floor beside tables, conveyer belts ran from one end of the room to an opening in the wall on the other end, continuing onward to some unknown destination. Barrels and boxes lined the outer walls, full of twine and packaging supplies. Seeing no access to a higher level, they moved on toward a doorway on the opposite end of the room. Adrianna noticed the footprints were overlaid a few times the closer they got to the doorway. She heard a scurrying behind her and spun around. A large rat ran across a table close by and down into a box. Sighing with relief, she remembered she needed to keep an eye behind them, just in case. She had to watch all of their backs.

As they neared the doorway, the agent on point motioned for them to get along the wall. He could see the second level from his vantage point.

Making sure it was clear, they entered the next room and immediately maneuvered themselves to the outer walls. As they stood, Adrianna could hear Miller muttering and ranting, angrily somewhere above them. A small office was positioned on top of the stairs, no walls, just the essentials. A small doorway led to another room Adrianna could barely see. From what she seen, mostly filing cabinets and papers.

Suddenly, something large was thrown against a wall inside the room and Sara shrieked. For a moment, Adrianna could see Miller inside. Garcia grabbed Adrianna's elbow, motioning for her to follow her. They all snuck back out of the room, careful not to be seen. Safely back on the other side of the wall, Adrianna mouthed to Carter "What now?"

Raising a finger, he reached for the walkie-talkie and radioed the teams in the back of the building. "Team Alpha, Team Bravo, copy?"

"Copy, sir. We're still in position."

"Copy. Do you have eyes on the target?"

"Negative, sir. There's a set of stairs outside that leads up to a room where we think the target is. Still no visual. Copy?"

"Copy that. Can you hear anything from your position?"

"Yes, sir. We can hear him inside the room, sir."

"Good. We have visual of him from our side. Hold your position. Copy?"

"Copy that, sir."

Agent Carter hunkered down close to Adrianna and the others while one of his agents kept an eye on the next room. "How do you want to do this, sir?" Garcia whispered.

He crouched there against the wall, running through the options. Adrianna watched him contemplate for a minute, but impatience was poking at her. "We can try to sneak up the stairs to him and hope we can catch him off guard, but there's a problem. Just about anything we do from this point, he's going to grab Sara and hide behind her. It happens quite often actually. No matter what we do, she could get hurt."

They were silent again, as if they were all praying it would work out okay. "What if I go in first?" Adrianna suggested.

"No. It's too dangerous."

"Come on, man. What part of this entire situation hasn't been dangerous? Come on. I can go out there by myself, holler at him to come out. Get his attention on me. If he thinks I came alone, maybe he'll let down his guard and come down by himself. And when I have him focused on me, your guys in the back can move in to get Sara and you all can surround him. We can take him down."

"It's risky, but it might work." Garcia muttered.

"It's a chance. Maybe the only one we got. What do you say Carter?" Adrianna asked.

He nodded his head in agreement and radioed the other teams. "Copy that, sir. We're in position."

"Copy. Wait for our signal."

"Okay." Adrianna whispered. She glanced at Garcia and turned toward the doorway. She slid over and peered around the wall and could see the door to the little room and heard Miller still inside. Standing, she slid her holster farther to her back and put her hands up in front of her before she stepped through the threshold, and into the next room. She watched the room off the office for any movement and walked to the center of the room.

"Miller! I've come to get my friend back! Come out!" she yelled.

A loud thump resounded from the room, and then she seen him come close to the door and peek around at her. "Put your hands up so I can see them!" he yelled back.

She tried to keep his focus on only her. "They are dumbass. Why don't you come out from there and see for yourself?"

"Dumbass? You bitch!" He wailed, as he came around to stand in the doorway. "Where's your cop buddies, huh? Are they the ones that told you to cut your hair?"

"You really think they were going to come with me to help me find Sara?" she scoffed. "They said they had to go by "the book". That actually told

me to stay where I was and let them do their jobs."
She added, pretending to be angry. She started
pacing around the room as she ranted, trying hard to
sell the illusion.

"They weren't going to come, so I did. I'm
not going to let my best friend be taken away by
some dumbass like you and do nothing about it. I
wasn't going to just sit around and let them do their
jobs. Ha! The cops haven't helped shit! They didn't
save me from The Staten Island Stalker. They didn't
kill Randal-what's-his-name when he came for me.
I did! *Their* job! Ha!" She glanced up at him. He
still stood in the doorway, but now fully exposed
himself, and she could see a pistol in his left hand.

"Their job. *I've* been doing their job! I
have! Like today. I drove all the way here, found a
map of the town, and figured out where you'd be
hiding. I did that! Not them!"

"So, you came alone?" he sneered as he
relaxed. "How did you find out where I was?" His
eyes fell over her bandage. "How does your arm
feel?" he smirked.

"That was easy. I knew you wouldn't be in
any of the houses. Surely, *The Staten Island Stalker*

would've told you that wasn't safe, or smart. So, it had to be another type of building. And since you and your friend, sorry, *late* friend," she stopped pacing and looked right up at him as his eye twitched in irritation. "Y'all prefer to hide out in old, abandoned warehouses covered in filth. So, I figured this was the best shot." She glanced at her bandage. "And I've been hurt worse. This is nothing."

His sweaty face reddened. "So, you found me. What now? What's your plan?" He smiled maliciously, baring his yellow and black rotten teeth.

"Well, actually, the correct word is *us*. You found *us*." Adrianna added, deliberately pissing him off. "I didn't just find *you*. I found you *and* my friend. She's here isn't she? I want to see her." Adrianna didn't wait for an answer. She walked briskly and deliberately up the stairs right to him.

"Stay back!" he screamed, as he backed up nervously.

"Why?"

"Because-because you can't be this close. You need to go back down there. Then I'll bring her out to show you."

"No."

"No?"

"Yes, no. I'm not walking back down those stairs without my friend." She took a step closer to him, seemingly to peer over his shoulder. "Let me see her."

"No. Not this way." Adrianna could see the wheels turning in his head.

"How then?" she asked, not wanting to push too much.

"Uh…" he started backing up again, farther into the room. Adrianna knew she was pushing too hard.

"Okay… How about I stand here, and you bring her out to me?" she stepped back and leaned against the rail. She felt her gun push against her back as she leaned on the rail and smiled a little.

Seeing her smile, a look of confusion filled his eyes. "What are you smiling at?"

"I'm... just thinking of Sara and the fun stuff we used to do together." She created quickly as she looked at the metal landing under her feet. "Go on. Go get her." She tried to remain calm and continue with the plan. The urge to tackle him and punch him in his disgusting face was starting to be difficult to resist.

"Okay…" he still looked confused. He stepped back again, farther into the doorway of the room. His gun held tightly in his hand.

What am I going to do? Adrianna thought. I've let this go too far. He won't let me into the room, and I have to be careful not to show him my back because he'll see my gun if he hasn't already. I can't let him get ahold of Sara. As soon as I got eyes on her, I have to act. But what do I do?

She peered quickly behind him, eyeing the other door on the other side of the long room. Glancing around, all she could see was filing cabinets. Suddenly, movement caught her eye, and she could see Sara's shoe move out from beside a cabinet. There she is! She glanced back at Miller, he was stepping back again, this time searching with his other hand for the doorknob. He was going to close the door behind him when he went in. Oh, hell no!

She tried to calm herself and stared intently at him. "Go on. Go get Sara and bring her to me."

"Okay… I'll be right back." He muttered cautiously. He took a final step back and turned around to close the door behind him.

In one brisk move, she lunged at him and grabbed him from behind. She grabbed his hand holding his gun and wrapped her other around his throat, pulling him backward, back towards the landing. He fought against her and tried to break free. She slammed his hand against the railing, as she tried to knock it out of his hand. Again, she slammed his hand, causing it to finally fall to their feet. Frantic, he tried to reach for it, so she kicked it off the landing to the floor below.

He instinctually reached for it, though he was unable to catch it, she took her chance and spun him around to face her. Immediately, she reared, and her fist crashed into his jaw. His knees buckled beneath him, and he laid haggard against the rail. Glancing into the other room, she could see men carry Sara out of the building and others clearing the area before heading in her direction. Turning, she saw the agents spill in from the other room, and Carter, Garcia, and Sam ran to her.

"Adrianna! Watch out!" Garcia screamed.

But Eddie Miller had snatched Adrianna's gun from her back and was pointing it at her as she spun around towards him. The gun rang out as she yelled in pain. Taking a quick breath, pissed off, she stood tall and kicked him square in his chest. He flipped backwards over the railing, his face covered with pain and confusion as he plummeted to the floor below. Men in tactical gear immediately swarmed him, cuffing him, and taking him to be detained outside in one of the cars. (FBI agent), (profiler), and Sam all ran to her.

"Oh my god! Are you okay?" Sam yelled.

Blood poured out of Adrianna's shoulder; her shirt already drenched. Wincing in pain, she grinned. "You know, I must be pretty bad at this if I'm always getting shot." She laughed. "But at least I'm a better shot than that bastard. Point blank range and he catches me in the shoulder?"

The group burst into laughter as they helped her down the stairs. They walked outside, and seen an ambulance already there tending to Sara. Upon seeing her friend approaching her covered in blood, Sara immediately collapses in tears.

"Are you okay?" she cried.

"Of course, I'm okay. I just got shot again." Adrianna laughed. Sara stared at her. "Look, you really think I was going to let that bastard get away with kidnapping you?"

"But you're hurt." Sara muttered.

"So?" Adrianna laughed. "After everything I've been through, a bullet's not going to stop me."

"I knew you would come, but I couldn't stop thinking about everything they did to you. I was so afraid he was going to-."

"Yeah, no, that's not going to happen. Besides, this one didn't have the smarts the other one did. He wouldn't have been able to do all those things." She lied. "Plus, you're a fighter Sara. You would've been able to fight him off. And I'm not ever going to let anyone do those things to you. Ever." Adrianna smiled at her, reassuringly.

Sara smiled back. The paramedics began working on Adrianna's gunshot wound. They were just stitching her up when an officer came over to Adrianna and the team.

"Sir?"

"Yes, deputy?"

"The suspect is complaining that he's hurt and wants to go to the hospital. He looks fine, but he has a big bloody knot on the back of his head. He might have a concussion. Should we take him to the hospital?"

"On the *back* of his head?" Adrianna asked, confused. "When I kicked him off, he landed on his front, not his back."

"Oh, no. That was from me." Sara interrupted. "When he tried to grab me the first time at the garage, I grabbed a heavy wrench and hit him in the head. I thought it'd knock him out, so I could get away, but it didn't. He just kind of stumbled, then he hit me. The next thing I knew, I was waking up in a truck and he was pulling in here."

Carter laughed and said, "You can have the paramedics check him out really quick to make sure he's not concussed, but he's going to jail. No less than four guards on him at all times and he stays in his cuffs. Matter of fact shackle him too. We're not taking any chances this time."

"Yes, sir." The deputy headed back to the car with the paramedics close behind.

"So," Adrianna said, standing. "What happens now?"

"For now, let's all just get back to the station." Sam smiled.

Book 2
Written by N L Hiser

<u>Forty-Four</u>

"**D** ad!**"** **Sara screamed as they** walked into the police station, and saw her dad sitting on a bench with his head in his hands.

He looked up abruptly, instantly bursting into tears upon seeing his daughter. "Sara!" he mumbled behind his cries. She ran to him, immediately crying into his shoulder.

"Dad!"

"I didn't know what to do. I was so scared. Are you alright? Are you hurt?"

"No, no, I'm fine, Dad. I'm fine. No more hurt than after a kickboxing class." Her dad continued to cry, overwhelmed with emotion. "They found me, Dad. Adrianna found me. I'm okay." She looked over at Adrianna and smiled.

Her dad finally raised his head, wiping away his tears. "Adrianna? Where is-?" His eyes settling on her a few feet away, and immediately noticed her blood-soaked clothes. "Oh my god! Adrianna! Are you alright?" he exclaimed.

She glanced at her shoulder, smiled, and went over to hug him. "I'm fine. I promise."

He embraced her, and the tears came again. "Thank you. Thank you for bringing back my girl. If anything had happened to her…"

"But nothing did." The women inserted.

Adrianna ushered Sara and her dad along with her to the conference room, as everyone was debriefed. A couple deputies gave her a look of disapproval, assumingly for bringing them in the room, but she didn't care. Sara and her dad had as much right to be there as Adrianna had. They needed to know that it was really over too.

They sat up arrangements for Carter and his team to escort Miller back to New York. S.W.A.T. was to stay with him until he was inside FBI headquarters in New York. No one was going to take any risks this time. He was to remain locked up at FBI headquarters jail until his arraignment, and then straight to prison in Southport where he'd be held for the rest of his life. Though he and his late partner killed and did other crimes in many states, everyone agreed that it was best to keep him in one place. Carter assured Adrianna that the judge would agree to it as well.

Adrianna left her contact information with Chief Malony in case they needed any more information for their paperwork. Since Sam and her both needed to get back to Staten Island, they decided to leave with the FBI in case anything happened on the way. They all started loading up their belongings and getting ready to go.

"Adrianna?" Sara's dad came outside, Sara right behind him.

"Hey."

"You're leaving?" Sara asked sadly.

"Not for long. I'm heading back to Staten Island with Sam. We'll be part of the convoy." She chuckled.

"But why? Everything's over. You can walk away from it now." Sara hugged her close.

"I know. We have to go back anyways. My truck's at Sam's house. And some of my things. And since we're all heading that way," she motioned toward the FBI agents. "we're just going to join the convoy. That way if anything happens on the way, we're there for extra backup."

"Oh...when will we see you again?"

"Soon. We're still planning on a mini-vacation to my place, right?" Adrianna smiled to Sara.

"Of course." Sara smiled.

"All this sort of interrupted the plans, but now we don't have to wait as long. Now, as soon as I get back and get all my things loaded up, I can come right back and get you. If you're still okay with that, that is." She looked questioningly at Sara's dad. She knew that after just getting her back, he might not be ready for her to leave.

"Of course. You rescued her." He laughed. "If she's safe with anyone, it's with you. Besides, I can use some peace and quiet for a while. Might even see if Ms. Charlette down the road needs help with anything around the house. I feel bad sometimes that she doesn't have anyone to help her out." He smiled crookedly.

The women laughed and hugged him. "I'm sure she would love your help, Dad."

"So, y'all spend some time together, and you get your stuff together. I'll text you if anything happens and as soon as we get into Staten Island. Depending on what time it is, I might stay the night and head out first thing in the morning. Y'all call me if you need anything, okay? And I'll see you both sometime early tomorrow."

"Awesome! Sounds good to me. Please be careful."

"We will."

Sam returned to the car then and smiled as he approached them. "Sam, it was nice to meet you finally. Adrianna told me so much about you, it was nice to put a face to the name." Sara smiled and shook his hand.

"And you, Sara. Adrianna told us a lot about you and your dad too. My wife will be sad she missed the chance to meet you two." He said, shaking her dad's hand. He turned to Adrianna, "You ready to go?"

"Yep." She hugged (Sara's dad) and gave him a kiss on the cheek. Then she hugged Sara, "I'll be back before you know it, I promise."

"Tomorrow then. Stay safe." Adrianna got in and closed the door.

"Tomorrow." She smiled. She nodded to Sam and they pulled out to follow the convoy. She waved back at Sara and her dad, a little sad to be saying goodbye again, but she was so happy that Sara was okay and that everything was good again.

"Are you okay?" Sam asked quietly as he drove.

"You know what? I think I am. For the first time in a long time."

Sam saw her smile and grinned, his eyes filled with joy. "Good. Really good."

Book 2
Written by N L Hiser

<u>Forty-Five</u>

Other than stopping once on the way out of town to fuel up on gas and snacks, the convoy went smoothly. They made it back to New York uneventfully, and watched as the rest of the convoy continued to Southport as they turned to head back to Staten Island and Sam's wife. As they neared the house, Adrianna got more excited to see Iris and Tiger. It was already dark by time they reached New York, so Adrianna made sure it was alright to stay another night with the Jones'.

When they finally pulled into the drive, they both let out a sigh of relief. Iris ran outside to meet them as soon as they pulled in, her eyes filled with tears. She hugged her husband tight and kissed him hello, before then pulling Adrianna into a long hug.

"I missed you both so much." She cried. "I was so worried when you all left."

"I know you were. You always are." Sam laughed. "But we're back. And Adrianna's going to stay the night tonight, so she can rest up before she leaves tomorrow." He smiled. "Is that okay?"

"Of course, it's okay." She laughed and smiled at Adrianna. "You don't have to ask, honey. He does, but you don't." she laughed again. "You can stay whenever you want. It's going to be sad seeing you go home." Her eyes fell.

"It won't be forever. Y'all are family now, and you both have helped me so much. I'll be back to visit again."

"Good." Sam said as he carried his things in behind them. "Because if we never saw you again, that'd be kind of hard for us to deal with. You're family to us, too."

Adrianna smiled, genuinely happy. "Well, I know it's a little late, but is anyone hungry?" Iris asked.

"Are you kidding? I've missed your cooking, babe." Sam smirked.

"I have to. There's not many people out there that can cook like you, Iris."

"Awe. You two…" The woman grinned ear to ear, blushing. "You two go get cleaned up and I'll get you some food ready."

"Thank you." Adrianna hollered after her as the woman strutted off to the kitchen. She glanced at Sam and they both giggled a bit. Adrianna headed up to the guest room. As soon as she entered the room, Tiger meowed loudly and ran to her from the bed. "Tiger! Oh! I missed you too, boy!" Adrianna kissed him on the top of the head as she picked him up and held him close. He headbutted her and rubbed his cheek against hers. "Awe! I love you to boy!"

Ten minutes later, they all converged on the dining room, Tiger in close pursuit. They sat and ate in silence, but for the kitty's constant purring at their feet. After they finished, they sat and drank some tea and talked, the women catching up on everything that had happened. Sam's phone rang, and his wife instantly looked over a little upset.

Sam stood and walked into the hallway to take the call. Adrianna tried to draw her attention away, but it didn't work very well. She could tell she was worried he'd need to leave again. Adrianna really hoped he wouldn't have to. A moment later, he returned to the table smiling.

"Don't worry. I'm not going into work. I was already going to call the Chief tomorrow and ask for a day off anyway, but he just gave me two." He laughed.

"Oh good." His wife smiled, reclining back in her chair. "So, that's why he called?"

"Oh, no. He knows you're here, Adrianna. And he wanted to make sure to let you know, they're holding a candlelight vigil for the victim's tomorrow night. He thought maybe you'd want to go."

"Oh…I don't know. I'm supposed to go pick up Sara tomorrow. I would like to, though. I'll text her." She got up and left the room for a minute. Instead of texting her and waiting for a response, she decided to just call. She answered on the second ring.

"Hey."

"Hey. I know it's late. I just have something I need to ask you really quick."

Sara laughed. "It's fine. Are you settled in for the night?"

"Yeah. But I just found out their holding a candlelight vigil for the victims tomorrow night. I was wondering…if you'd mind waiting one more day for me to come pick you up. I think I should go."

"Of course, I don't mind. I think you should go to. Not just to support the others, but to get some closure for yourself to. It could be good for you."

"Yeah, I think so too. And then I'll head your way first thing the next morning. Is that alright?"

"Sounds good to me. Plus, it'll give me one more day with my dad before leaving."

"True. Though he did seem pretty excited to spend some time with *Ms. Charlette* down the road." she giggled.

Sara's laughter filled the speaker. "Oh, you have no idea. Just wait until you see him."

She smiled. "Okay, well tell him I said hi, and I'll text you in the morning. Goodnight, Sara."

"I will. Goodnight, Adrianna. Talk to you tomorrow."

She hung up and returned to the dining room. "Okay, I'm going to the vigil." She announced upon seeing the Jones'. "I'm going to clean these up really quick and get some sleep. It's been a long day." She grabbed her dishes quickly and took them to the kitchen before Iris could argue and washed them. She told the Jones' goodnight and headed upstairs to her room with Tiger close at foot.

She took a quick shower and put some food in Tigers bowl, then curled up in bed. Tiger came up and laid next to her bandaged and sore arm and purred against her. Before long, she had drifted off to sleep, and for the first night in a long time, she actually rested.

Forty-Six

The next day, she woke calm and rested. When she opened her eyes, Tiger still laid beside her being a loving boy. Now on his back and sprawled out, he laid with a content grin on his face. "Good morning, silly boy." She stretched and felt her sore arm, grinning past the pain. What's the odds of being shot twice in the same arm? She wondered.

Standing, she stretched her back and got dressed. I need to make sure I get back to exercising when I get back home, she thought. But for now, this is nice. She gave Tiger a few treats, cleaned herself up, headed downstairs.

Thinking she was the first awake, she walked into the kitchen to start some coffee, but Iris was already there pouring a cup. Adrianna giggled. "Good morning."

"Good morning, dear. How'd you sleep?"

"Great, actually. Thanks." She took the cup she offered and poured in some cream and sugar. Stirring, she added, "Hmm, do you have a computer I could use?"

"Of course. It's in the study. This way."

"Thanks. I appreciate it." She followed her into a room down the hall. Iris turned on the computer and sat down, waiting for it to load for her. "It'll take me just a minute. I left my laptop at home and I've been thinking about something I want to order."

"Oh, take your time, dear. What are you ordering? I love to online shop. Sam hates it though." She laughed.

Adrianna giggled. "Actually, it's just a little something for the house. Since Sara's coming to stay for a week or so, a little mini-vacation, I thought I'd get something that could help us enjoy it. See?" she pointed at the screen after taking bringing up the site.

"Oh, yeah. She'll love it. Plus, it's something you can enjoy all the time. I wish we had one."

"Yeah. I ordered from a place pretty local to my house. Cheaper and quicker." She giggled. "Done. It'll be delivered tomorrow evening."

"That's good. Quick shipping. Nice."

"Yep." She giggled. "It's going to be fun."

"I'm so happy for you girls. You need some relax and refresh time, and that's always best with a good friend."

"Absolutely." They could hear Sam whistling as he walked down the stairs. Giggling to each other, they headed back to the kitchen. Adrianna sat down in one of the chairs by the window, sipping her coffee, while Iris started breakfast. Tiger strolled into the kitchen with Sam and jumped up onto Adrianna's lap for some attention.

"Good morning, ladies." Sam serenaded. Watching Adrianna, he added, "You know, I'm fairly certain that cat was meant to be with you. He sure does love you." He chuckled. "Little punk tried to trip me coming off the stairs."

Adrianna giggled. "Yeah, I love this little kitty too. I just hope he does well on long car rides."

The Adrianna Swift Series
Swift Snake

"Oh, I'm sure he'll do fine." Iris reassured her as they walked into the dining room with their plates. "Maybe you can get him one of those harness's that hook to the seat belt. They make them for dogs, so maybe they have them for cats too. If nothing else, it'll help to ease your mind while you're driving."

"Yeah, that's a good idea. Thank you. I'll see about it today." Sitting down, she added. "Sam, do you know what time the vigil is going to start?"

"It's supposed to be right before dark. A couple people's going to go up and say a few words, and then everyone's going to light their candles as the sun sets. They didn't say an actual time, but I figure with this time of year... I'd say around about six-thirty, seven o'clock."

"Okay, cool. Have you heard anything from the FBI? Everything still going alright? Is he locked up tight?"

"Last I heard, he is. I wouldn't worry about him anymore, Adrianna. I don't think the FBI is taking any chances this time. Plus, I made sure they put both of us on the list to be notified immediately if anything does happen."

"I just wanted to make sure. I'm not worried. Not a lot anyways. I just don't want him to have the chance to hurt anyone ever again."

"He won't."

Taking a big breath, she breathed out and continued. "You're right. I thought about whether I should go talk to him. I sort of feel like I should, but I can't really think of why. I mean, I don't need any more closure than knowing he's locked away. I'm going to the vigil tonight out of respect for the victims, and to celebrate the lives of my daughter and husband. And to celebrate Alex's life. He lost his life protecting me and was one of the only reasons I've made it this far. That's enough closure for me."

"So, why do you feel like you need to go talk to that bastard for?"

"I really don't know. It's like a gut feeling. Like I forgot something. It doesn't feel like it was super important, but I still can't shake the feeling."

"Maybe, it's just, I don't know, residual feelings? You've dealt with so much, physically, and emotionally, over the last year or so. It's not going to just all be resolved and never effect you again. It takes time. Maybe that's all it is?" Iris suggested.

"Maybe you're right." Adrianna muttered as she sipped her coffee.

"You know what? I have to go out shopping for a few things today. How about you come with me? We can get one of those harness's for Tiger, and do a little girls shopping? What do you say? Just get out for a while and have some fun."

Adrianna smiled, "That sounds great."

"Good. You ladies have fun and I'll just sit around here and-."

"Take care of a few things here at the house that need done?" Iris jokingly suggested, cutting him off.

"I can't wait." He muttered, sitting back in his chair. Adrianna tried hard not to laugh.

"Good. The list is on the fridge."

They finished and cleaned up breakfast, before they headed out to the store. Texting Sara a 'good morning', she grabbed her things and walked downstairs. "Bye-bye, Tiger. I'll be back in a little bit. Be good and I'll bring you back something special." Adrianna said to Tiger, scratching his head. He purred loudly and meowed to her as she went out the door.

Book 2
Written by N L Hiser

Forty-Seven

It had been a really long time since Adrianna had went out shopping with a girlfriend. It ended up being a pretty great day. She bought Tiger quite a few things, got some bathing suits, and a few other things. They ran a few errands after lunch and headed back to the house. Walking in, they had found Sam asleep on the couch. Giggling, they went about their way.

Now, hours later, Adrianna stepped out of the bathroom from a hot shower, walking around her things she had packed up for the trip tomorrow. She would leave out early in the morning to head to Petersburg to Sara. And then on to Luray and home. As the hours trickled by, she got more excited for the coming days. She pulled on her outfit for the candlelight vigil and sat on the bed, not really thinking of anything in particular. Instead, just enjoying the peaceful moment.

Half an hour later, Adrianna and the Jones' were in the car and headed to the ceremony. Everyone was quiet, mulling over their thoughts. The last time they all went to a ceremony, it was Alex's funeral. This time, she thought, it's about celebrating life and remembering those we've lost. Tonight, it's about giving closure to everyone affected by two horrible men. Tonight would mark a new page in everyone's lives.

As they pulled into the parking lot, she texted Sara to let her know they were at the vigil and she would let her know afterwards how it went. She got a text back almost immediately saying 'good luck. I'm here if you need me.' They walked over to the park where they could see everyone gathering.

Suddenly, Adrianna started to feel overwhelmed with emotion. So many people were affected by these two men. So many. And these were only the ones from Staten Island. She remembered the board on the wall, the map with all the pushpins everywhere they had attacked, tortured, killed, robbed, and hurt. So many... Tears started welling in her eyes. It's so incredibly heart breaking, she thought.

Her thoughts were suddenly interrupted as she walked past a small group talking and someone said, "Oh my god! It's her." Suddenly, whispering could be heard starting from one end of the large gathering to the next.

The Jones' came closer to her, and Iris wrapped her arm through hers. "Do you want to leave? Just say the word and we'll go." She whispered.

"No, it's okay. I should have expected at least one person to recognize me. It's fine. I want to stay." She uttered.

"Alright. Just let us know if you do." Sam whispered. His wife let go off her arm, but they stayed close.

A small bell chimed somewhere in front, drawing everyone's attention. She and the Jones' moved closer to see what was happening. A young woman stood on the top step of the gazebo, waiting for everyone to quiet down.

"Hello! Thank you all for coming to this candlelight vigil in honor of those taken by Randall Wright and Edward Miller. My name's Erica. My brother and his family were murdered by the two, a year and a half ago. I know a lot of us don't really want to go into detail about what happened, and the sun is setting. So, I'd like to bring up our mayor at this time. Mayor Smith?"

"Hello, everyone. You all know who I am, so I'm not going to get into that. Tonight, we are gathered in honor of those loved ones lost in this horrific event. But we're not the only ones effected by this. These two men hurt many others in many other states as well. They took a lot of lives, but in this horrendous act, they brought all of us around the country, together. So, before we light the candles, I'd like to invite any of you up here that would like to take a moment and talk. So, at this time, the stage is yours." The mayor stepped back from the microphone.

Everyone glanced around to each other, most too afraid to stand up in front of everyone. A few looked at Adrianna. She took a deep, steadying breath and stepped up the gazebo.

"Umm…Hi. I know many of you have already realized who I am. For those of you that haven't, my name is, or was, Katherine Davidson. I go by Adrianna Swift now. I am the only surviving victim." A tear slid down her cheek. Refusing to give up, she pushed forward. "Victim. I still don't like that word. But it's the truest one. Over a year ago, the Staten Island Stalker, now found to be Randall Wright, broke into my home, and murdered my daughter and husband. He then knocked me out and took me away; to torture me. Thankfully, the police found him before he could kill me. But he had already done so much damage." Tears flowed freely from her now, but she cleared her throat and persisted to tell her story.

After being released from the hospital, I discarded with the remnants of my life, and ran. I thought, if I could run far enough away, he could never find me. I had horrible nightmares and started having anxiety and panic attacks. Eventually, after making some really great friends, I grew stronger and learned how to deal with the life I had left. I knew he was still going to come after me, so I got prepared. He escaped the prison he was in and did come after me. That was a big mistake on his part. I killed him that night, so he couldn't hurt anyone else ever again. But not before he killed one of the best men I've ever known. He died protecting me. It was after that, that we learned he had a partner. I came back here to try to find him and stop him. They had already destroyed my life, and so many other's lives."

We learned who they were, where they had been, how many other lives they took before they even got here to Staten Island. He took my best friend, trying to hurt me and draw me out. That was a mistake too. Now, he's locked up and never getting out. I promise you all, that this man will never hurt anyone or take anyone's family away again."

I promise you. I am so sorry they hurt you all. I am sorry for everyone they took from this life. But it's over. We can take back our lives again. We are in charge of our own lives. Never again will either of these men, ever hurt us again. Never again will they come in the night and destroy us. Never again. Now is our time to move on. We have to live for them. Our loved ones cannot live and do the things they thought they were going to do. Our children will never grow old, will never have families, or grow up to be princesses anymore." She paused, thinking of her baby girl. Her princess. "But we are still here. We have a life to live still. And no one is going to take that from us. No one. We are in charge now." She wiped the tears from her eyes and took a deep breath as she tried to steady her nerves.

"We have to live our lives for *them* now. They cannot, and will not, have died in vain. Instead, we are going to go forth and have a life worth living. It's still going to hurt. I lost my parents when I was young. It still hurts. That part never really stops. We'll always have the scar from this. But we'll still heal. We'll breath, and we'll move on. And every day, it'll be a little easier. Every time we think about them, and remember, it'll hurt just a little less. But we carry them along with us in life. They are always with us. Always. So, let's show them how great we can be." She motioned for the Jones' to join her. They came up and stood beside her, the first speaker and Mayor joining them. She took out a lighter and continued.

"Tonight, as we light these candles and go into the rest of our lives, let us remember our loved ones. Not any of the bad memories. Just remember the good. Tonight, we remember the greatest things about our loved ones, our greatest memories of them, our love for them, and their love for us. Tonight, we celebrate their lives. This is for them." She lit her candle. "For my husband, daughter, and one of the best men I've ever known."

She lit the Jones' candles with hers, "For Alex." they smiled, tears running down their cheeks. They lit the mayors and the speaker's, Erica's. From there, they lit other's candles and it continued on until every candle was lit. Everyone saying the name of who they lost. Everyone cried, and smiled, as they remembered.

Forty-Eight

The next morning, she woke up at six o'clock and jumped in the shower to start her day. An hour later, she was dressed and carrying her things to her truck, packing them into the cab. After her last trip upstairs to gather Tiger and his things, she took a couple minutes to stretch. Traveling so much in one day, not stretching would have really hurt her come nightfall. She toted Tigers things to the truck, leaving him in his carrier at the door. When she turned around to go back inside, the Jones' were at the door.

"Good morning!"

"Good morning, Adrianna. I didn't realize you would be leaving so early." Iris looked a little sad.

"I was just putting everything in the truck. Tiger and I were going to wait until after y'all woke up. We wouldn't have left without saying goodbye." She smiled.

"Oh, well in that case, how about some breakfast before you hit the road?"

"Sounds great." She hadn't intended on staying for breakfast, but Adrianna knew they would be upset if she didn't, so she closed the door behind her and followed the Jones' to the kitchen, toting Tiger along with her. Putting him down in the dining room, she followed them to the kitchen to help make breakfast.

"We...sort of got you a surprise." Sam winked. He nodded toward the breakfast table.

She looked over and smiled as she seen a large gift basket on the table. "Oh my gosh. Y'all didn't have to do this."

"Oh, we know. But we couldn't resist. I mean, who knows how long it'll be until we get to see you again. And you're part of the family now. We couldn't let you go without a little something." Iris's smile didn't reach her eyes, instead tears welled up and threatened to fall.

"This is little?" Adrianna raised a brow, jokingly.

"Obviously." Sam said, trying to keep a straight face. The doorbell rang, and Sam went to see who it was, laughing.

"How about some coffee?" Iris remarked, leaving Adrianna questioning what the woman was up to. Or if she was just upset.

Adrianna browsed through the items in the basket. A large combat knife with belt holster, a can of pepper spray, some snacks and sodas, a couple of new movies, a framed photo of the Jones', a small bag of treats and toys for Tiger, a small photo of Alex, and an emergency kit for the truck. Adrianna laughed. "You two know me *pretty* well."

"Well, we wanted to make sure you were protected on the road." Sam replied as he returned to the room. He held a few bags of food in his hands. "We ordered some breakfast when we heard you get up this morning."

She gasped in astonishment and smiled gleefully as tears welled up in her eyes. "I'm going to miss y'all so much. Thank you; for everything. I don't know what I would've done without the two of you. You both are incredibly special to me and I'll never forget what you've done for me." A tear slid down her cheek.

"We're going to miss you too." Sam drew Iris close to him. "It won't be the same around here without you."

Adrianna giggled a little, "Maybe that'll be a good thing."

They chuckled at that and took their coffee's and food to the dining room table to eat. They ate and laughed over the next hour, enjoying each other's company. She then cleaned up and carried the basket over to Tiger, knowing it was time for her to go.

"We know." The Jones' said, when she turned to them. They followed her out to her truck and waited while she put the basket and Tiger in the front seat. Adrianna jumped in and moved the basket over and brought Tiger out of the carrier and latched his harness to the pet seat belt she had bought the day before. Moving the rest to the back seat or floorboard and out of Tigers way, she then jumped down out of the truck and gave the Jones' a big hug goodbye.

She then climbed back into the driver's seat, closed the door, hooked her seatbelt, and tried her best not to cry. She turned over the engine and said "Goodbye!" to the Jones' as she pulled out of the driveway, onto the road, and away. She could see them in her rearview mirror, still watching and waving.

When she got to the stop sign at the end of the street, she quickly texted Sara that she was on her way before she drove off. She took a deep breath and smiled. It's going to be a great day, she thought, as she glanced over to Tiger standing on the passenger seat watching the world go past his window.

Book 2
Written by N L Hiser

<u>Forty-Nine</u>

S he arrived in Petersburg to pick up Sara a few hours later. Texting her that she was in town and would be there soon, she smiled, happy to soon be seeing her again. They pulled into a spot in front of the house ten minutes later. When the truck stopped, Tiger jumped down do the floorboard to use the litter box.

Giggling, she said, "I'm glad you're doing so well on the trip, Tiger." She hurried and cleared a spot on the small seat in the cab and pushed over everything in the floorboard in front of it. She'd have to strap Tiger to that seat for the rest of the trip. Hoping he wouldn't mind, she smiled as he jumped back up on the seat and curled up for a nap.

"Adrianna! You're here!" Sara exclaimed, running down the porch steps and over to her window.

"Hey!" she climbed out of the truck and hugged her. "Yeah, we finally made it."

"*We?*" Sara asked, raising a brow. Adrianna pointed inside the truck. "Aww! He's so cute!"

"I'm glad you think so. I was afraid you might not have liked cats."

"Oh, who doesn't like cats?" Sara laughed. "When did you get him?"

"He was Alex's. When we went to get his uniform for his funeral, we found Tiger. We didn't even know he had a cat. So, I adopted him."

"Aww. So cute!" she leaned over and scratched his furry head.

"Yeah, he is. You ready to go?"

"Yep. Help me grab my bags." They went in and grabbed her bags, packing them into the cab of the truck.

"Where's your dad?"

Sara giggled. "Getting his hair cut."

"Oh." Adrianna laughed.

"Yeah, I'm just going to text him that we're leaving." She texted her dad while Adrianna used the bathroom. A couple minutes later, they were all set up in the truck and ready to hit the road.

They stopped at a drive-thru and picked up some lunch on their way out of Petersburg. They laughed and chatted about everything that had happened in the last couple days since Adrianna had headed back to Staten Island.

Book 2
Written by N L Hiser

Fifty

They drove into Luray around **dinner** time, stopped to pick up take-out, groceries, and a couple other things before they headed to the house. They pulled into her driveway, pausing for a second to reach and grab the mail. As they pulled up to the house, they noticed a truck parked in front and seen men getting out.

"What's this? Were you expecting anybody?" Sara asked, suddenly worried.

"Yep!" Adrianna laughed. "They called while I was in the store saying they were five minutes away, so I just asked them to wait on us to get here." She jumped down out of the truck and ran over to the men.

"Hey, guys. Thanks for waiting."

"No problem, ma'am. We only had to wait for a minute or two."

"Good. Do you mind putting it right over there by the side of the house?"

"No, ma'am. Not at all. Would you like us to hook it up for you?"

"Please. We just got back from out of town and still need to unload the truck, so you'd be helping me out a lot."

"No problem at all, ma'am. And before we leave, I'll show you how to do it yourself for the future. It only takes five minutes."

"Awesome! I really appreciate it."

She returned to her truck, where Sara was already out and putting Tiger in his carrier. "What did you order?"

"A hot tub."

"What?"

"Yeah, I ordered us a hot tub. We'll be able to use it anytime, but I figured it'd be a nice little something for the next week or two while you're here."

"Are you kidding? That's awesome! Can we use it tonight?"

"Oh yeah. They're going to hook it up for me while we unload the truck. By time we eat and unpack, I think it should be ready to go."

"Hell yeah!" Sara laughed and helped Adrianna take everything inside.

They unloaded everything and Adrianna went outside to talk to the hot tub guys and tipped them while Sara was busy unpacking upstairs. By nine o'clock, everything was unpacked, Tiger was settled in and happy, and the hot tub was finally, officially hot enough. They clambered in and sunk deep into the water, both visibly relaxing.

"So... how are you feeling? Now that everything is over."

"Good. And glad it is finally over." Adrianna sighed as she let the water warm her.

"That's good. I know you don't really want to think about it right now. Maybe ever. But you haven't really gave yourself time to grieve."

"I know. And I will. I could feel it start to actually hit me the second we got here. After running for a year, and then Alex... I'm just glad it's over." She watched the stars above them for a second before continuing. "I miss them. Even my husband."

"I know, Hun. And that's okay. You still loved him. He was your family, no matter what issues y'all were having. Whatever way you feel about it, that's healthy. As long as you still allow yourself to feel."

"Yeah. I'll be okay. It's just going to take a while to deal with everything that's happened."

"Of course." Sara smiled at her in her usual supportive way.

"I'm glad I have you in my life. I don't know what I'd do without you."

"You'd be bored, of course." Sara laughed. Adrianna grinned at her, knowing how true it was.

"Oh, I just realized. Did you ever text Sam and his wife to tell them we made it?" Sara asked suddenly.

"Yeah. Otherwise they'd worry." She poured them both a shot of whiskey, courtesy of Sara, and sat the bottle on the table.

"I figured they would." Sara twirled her hand in the water. "Hey, did y'all ever find out who was helping the stalker guy deliver those letters or if it was the partner all along?"

"No...I forgot about that." Adrianna replied, perplexed. "I mean, someone must have helped them from inside the prison, right?"

"I'd think so."

"I'll ask Sam to look into it tomorrow. Tonight, let's just relax. I'd rather not think about that guy again, anytime soon."

"So, what do you want to do? I'm here for the next two weeks. Got any plans?"

Adrianna smiled and winked. "Maybe a few..."

Book 2
Written by N L Hiser

<u>Fifty-One</u>

Edward Miller sat in his cell, brooding over his defeat. "I can't believe that bitch got one up on me! I can't believe I'm now rotting in this filth, and she's out there probably smiling and happy." He snapped.

She killed Wright, put me in prison, and gets to live on with a happy life? It's total bullshit! It's not fair! Wright would be so pissed at me. He'd be so mad that I lost and let her go. She was supposed to die! She was supposed to! Not him!

I'll find a way to make things right. I will. I will.

I'll make sure that bitch dies.

"No, you won't." an eerie voice said from behind him.

The Adrianna Swift Series
Swift Snake

"W-what?"

"No-you-won't."

"Who are you?" he whined.

"You don't recognize my voice, Eddie?"

"Oh my god! No!"

"Yes!"

"No! It can't be you! She killed you!"

"Yes, she did. And it's all your fault!"

"No! No! I promise! I'll make it up to you! I'll kill her! I'll kill her for you!"

"No!" the voice bellowed. "No, you won't! You can't! You are too stupid to be able to best her! You're pathetic! You are filth!" it screamed.

"Please! Please! I'm not stupid. I can do it."

"No, you can't. You don't have it in you. You were never as good as me. You should die! You will die!"

"No! Please! Don't! Please! No!" Miller begged.

Book 2
Written by N L Hiser

"Do it!"

"Please! Please, don't make me! Please!"

"Do…it…now." The voice reverberated in his head.

He clamped his hands over his ears. "No! Please! Stop!"

"Do it! Do it- NOW!" the voice yelled.

Edward Miller stood on his bed, crying. Stripping off his jumpsuit, he wrapped it around the bars of his cells and then around his neck. His whimpering filled the cellblock as he begged one last time.

"Do it!"

He collapsed and hung, his neck snapping against the weight. His body swayed into the bed with a loud thud.

"Yes! Ha! Ha! Ha!" the eerie voice trailed out of the cell and down the quiet cell block. The only noise left, the creaking of the clothe tied to the bars, and the whimpering cries from a lifeless man.

Book 2
Written by N L Hiser

The Adrianna Swift Series
Swift Snake

Book 2
Written by N L Hiser

For anyone hurting from losing a loved one, you got this. We carry them with us as we live our lives. Choose to live. For them. For you. You are stronger than you know.

"Breath and carry on."

-Aunt Missy,

The Adrianna Swift Series

Book 2
Written by N L Hiser

For other titles written by N L Hiser, and to subscribe to my free newsletter to stay updated on my future and current works, click subscribe on my website at https://nlhiserwrites.com.

Follow N L Hiser @ nlhiserwrites on Instagram and YouTube.

Book 2
Written by N L Hiser

Look for **Lost Star** on Amazon and anywhere digital books are sold, October 1, 2021. This is book one of the **Tale of Two Hearts Series**, a new adult high fantasy series.

Look for **Feeding Fear** on Amazon and anywhere digital books are sold, October 1, 2021. This is book one of the **Miss Webmaker's Collection**, a horror short story collection.

Stay connected on YouTube, Instagram, and nlhiserwrites.com for updates on these books and more.

Buy Adrianna Swift Series merch on teespring.com/stores/nlhiser-writes.

N L Hiser is a 33-year-old mother who enjoys spending her free time hiking, fishing, doing crafts, and having random dance parties with her daughter in their West Virginian home.

Book 2
Written by N L Hiser

Made in the USA
Columbia, SC
29 March 2021